BACKGROUND NOISE

A Novel About Twice-Exceptionality

SUSAN LARSEN KRAUSE

With Alexander Lee Hampton and David Carter Hampton

Published by BACKGROUND NOISE BOOKS
backgroundnoisebooks.com

ISBN: 1546495851
ISBN-13: 978-1546495857

Illustrations by Haley Pepper Photography

Book design by Editsmith
editsmith.ontrapages.com

EDITSMITH

FOR MY PARENTS

"If you have made mistakes, even serious mistakes, you may have a fresh start any moment you choose, for this thing we call "failure" is not the falling down, but the staying down."
—Mary Pickford

CONTENTS

CHAPTER 1

STUFF WE NEED

Inside my brain, a war is raging. It's not your typical war. This is a war of words and ideas. This is a thinking war. It's a war that I am in by myself, and I've surrendered. It's over. The words win.

Enough being lazy.

You aren't even trying.

Don't you care?

Did you hear what I said?

What is your problem?

You are a terrible boy.

Here's how it ends: flaming arms reach up through the rooftop and grab for the stars. The house crackles and sparks. Sirens and shouting and dizzying lights from the emergency vehicles and water all swirl together. Mom is crying. Dad is somewhere else. It's unbelievably hot. Way hotter than a usual Phoenix summer and that's saying something. Even the pavement turns gooey in a Phoenix summer. People fry eggs on the hoods of their cars. They use hot mitts on their steering wheels.

I wish I were somewhere else.

A firefighter asks me questions. Am I okay? Where was I when the smoke detector sounded? What was I doing when the fire started?

I don't answer. I can't answer. I keep my hands in my pockets. He checks me over to see if I need to go the hospital. I'm counting the fast beats of my heart, and I can't speak. Not now. Maybe not ever.

Mom and I step back until we are flat against the fence of the neighbor's house across the street. Mom is standing close to me, tears running down her cheeks. She has one arm around my shoulders, and it feels like a burning log. I want to push it off, but I know that would make her even more upset. Once she finds out the truth, she probably won't ever feel the same about me, so I just stay put. Dad's sitting on a boulder in our neighbor's yard, his face buried in his hands. He doesn't watch any of this. Maybe he's peeking out through his fingers, but I can't tell.

I'm still counting my heartbeats. In fifteen more heartbeats, he'll come over to us, I tell myself. I count out fifteen rapid beats, but he doesn't move.

He's surrendered, too.

My hands search my pockets for the small coil of wire. A polished carbonate stone. A root beer bottle cap. I twist the wire tight around my finger until it hurts from lack of blood flow and wait for this moment to end. One hundred more heartbeats and this will be over.

But it doesn't end quickly. Even though I've lost, this war is everlasting.

We drive to a motel and Mom gets us a room. We're the only ones around except for the hotel clerk and a security guard. Dad is supposed to meet us here after he stops for things we need since we couldn't go into the burning house to get our toothbrushes. Mom watches anxiously out the lobby window while the hotel clerk runs her credit card.

"We smell like smoke," she says softly. The clerk smiles but doesn't say anything. I don't say anything. I add a matchbook from the lobby desk to my shirt pocket. A little token from the Sun Valley Motel to remind me what an awful thing I've done. Finally, we have a card key and Mom and I go to a room that faces the parking lot. Her hands are still shaking. She slides opens the heavy, dusty gold curtains and sits at the small table next to a yellow lamp, waiting for Dad.

"I'm going to take a shower. Watch for Dad, okay?" She hugs me, and I stiffen, not even taking my hands out of my pockets.

"Jeremy, you okay?"

I don't answer. Don't even look at her. She'll see the truth on my face. She sighs and leaves me there by the window. I sit on the edge of the bed and wait for the rumbling sound of Dad's silver diesel truck, which has one bumper sticker that reads, "My zombie ate your honor student."

The next day I sleep until late in the morning. I look over at the next bed, and it's empty. I check the bathroom, but both Mom and Dad are gone. The gold curtains are closed. When I pull them open, I am surprised that it's very bright outside. I quickly shut them again. For a moment, I hope it is just a nightmare, but I'm in a strange place, so it's not over. I get a drink of water out of the bathroom sink, but it tastes like chlorine, so I spit it out. I look around the room for something to eat. There's nothing. I go back to the bed and sit, wearing my clothes from yesterday. I still smell like smoke.

Mom's shadow appears walking by the window and opens the door. She has bags of stuff from GetMor4Less that she spills onto the bed.

"Eat something."

There's a box of powdered sugar donuts, some bananas, and apple juice boxes. She bought me two plain royal blue t-shirts with pockets on the front, two pairs of black nylon shorts with elastic waistbands and pockets, a package of black cotton boxers and a pair of black flip-flops. A toothbrush and a comb and a pair of scissors. I sit on the bed to eat a donut while Mom cuts the tags out of the t-shirts and shorts and underwear.

"They didn't have the socks you like, and I don't dare buy shoes without you there to try them on, so just flip flops for now."

I don't move. She sits down next to me and kisses me on the head, which I hate. I pull away.

"You should go shower," she says.

The first thing I do is take everything out of my pockets and put it on the counter. After I finish my shower, I put the stuff in the pockets of my new clothes. The wire and bottle cap go in the left pocket. The carbonate goes in the right. The matchbook from the hotel lobby goes in the pocket on my t-shirt. I come out of the bathroom and give Mom my smelly, smoky clothes which she bundles up in a plastic bag and puts outside the hotel room door, with hers, next to the garbage.

Just then her phone buzzes. It's a text message.

"Is it Dad?" My voice is froggy with the first words I have spoken since last night.

She picks up the phone and reads the message. Then she puts it down again, carefully, like it might explode.

"Mom?"

"Wrong number." Her voice is different. Her voice says I shouldn't ask any more questions.

Her voice says Dad isn't coming at all.

CHAPTER 2

THE GAME

Mom and I go back to the house, even though the fire captain told us to stay away. All that is left is charred and black. Orange traffic cones block the drive, and red caution tape wraps from palm tree to palm tree, encircling the house. Signs stuck to the cones and the trees say Danger: Do Not Enter. The house is wrapped in red and orange: a flashing "STAY AWAY" warning if I ever saw one.

I don't want to be here, but Mom wants me to help her look through what is left. She thinks she might be able to save something. She has optimistically packed cardboard boxes in the back of the car to fill with anything salvageable. Instead, Mom and I sit in the car and stare at the black sticks of our house gift wrapped in caution tape. Going inside is impossible. There isn't an inside left. There isn't stuff to save.

We can't live here anymore.

I look over at the boulder where I last saw Dad.

"Let's just go."

My stomach feels sick. Mom nods her head, and we drive away from the scene. It's the last time I see my house.

I only ever live two ways inside my head. Most of the time it's a battle I'm fighting alone. I'm under attack by words, numbers, song lyrics, Minecraft music, movie lines, memories. I'm in the middle of the world's largest and loudest pizza arcade nightmare, with every game playing at full volume, every light bright and exploding, every kid screaming to be heard over the other kids. That's the noisy part. The other way I live inside my head is folded into a little box. I can't see the lights or hear the noise from inside my box. The lights and noise are still there, but for a little while, it's quiet and dark. I imagine being covered by a heavy blanket of stars, floating in space, which is very cold. I wrap myself up and count my heartbeats. Eventually, I sleep.

I'm there now. I'm not ever coming out; no matter how much Mom begs me to talk to her.

We go back to the motel room, and I crawl into the bed and pretend to sleep, while Mom makes phone calls asking strangers if we can see the inside of their apartments. When she has a list of people who said yes, she sits on the bed next to me and asks if I want to come with her. I stay behind. I'm not in the mood to meet new people and see new places today. She gives me a ten-dollar bill for a hamburger at Dave's Burger Joint, which is next to the motel.

After she leaves, I go outside and look around. It's a small motel with a patch of trees and a swimming pool. There are a few people in the pool and a bunch of little kids splashing around in the kiddie pool. The temperature is 106° F. I consider climbing up from a bench to a shade structure which has perfect access to the roof of the hotel. I like being on rooftops, but anything over 85° F makes the surface too hot for my skin. My bedroom-that-was, I could climb out of the window and sit on a blanket I kept nearby and watch the whole neighborhood. I want to be on the roof now so I can see everything, but one of the moms at the pool looks at me weird. By weird I mean she is sending me a warning. I know your kind. Get lost.

I go Dave's Burger Joint. There's a tiny bit of hope that I'll see Dad there because it's his favorite place for coffee. It's cool inside, and Dave's has a climbing wall and a cargo net and tunnels that are attached to a structure called Dave's Tree House that isn't anything like a tree house. It's not as good as being on the roof, but it doesn't sear the skin off my shins. I climb up the slide and through the tunnels until I'm at the very top. I like to sit in one spot and watch. I'm not moving, so the little kids ignore me and crawl right by. Sometimes one will mistake me for the tunnel wall and place a hand on my knees to steady himself. I'm not interested in the kids who just cruise on by. It's the kid that's going to stop and ask questions: that's the kid I'm playing with. The one who figures out that this is a game.

The first kid to notice me is a little boy with red hair. He makes eye contact and giggles as he's crawling past me. I cross my eyes and stick out my tongue, and he squeals and crawls away faster. Every time he comes back he tries to sneak past and giggles at my goofy face. Eventually, he creeps closer and pokes me, and I come to life and wave my arms over my head and make monster sounds.

I stay there as kids come and go. It's easier to be around little kids than kids my age. Little kids don't think there is anything wrong with me at all.

I hear Mom's voice calling as she's standing with a Dave's person who is holding a mop. Mom waves me down.

She hugs me tight as soon as I'm off the slide.

"Jeremy, have you been here all day?" She asks in her talking quiet but yelling voice. I push her away because hugs are not my thing. She knows that but hugs me all the time anyway.

"Did you eat anything?" I slowly reach into my pocket and pull out the ten-dollar bill. She holds out her hand. We go to the counter to buy me a plain burger with ketchup only and a vanilla milkshake.

"What did you do up there?"

I don't look at her because I'm checking my hamburger to make sure they got it right. Was I up there all day? I have no idea what time it is.

She taps my hand that is resting on my burger and asks, "Jeremy, did you hear me?"

"I don't know. I don't know if it was all day."

"I found us an apartment. I think you'll like it. You get your own room with a balcony. It's on the second floor."

Mom keeps talking even though I don't respond. Her voice becomes a hum inside my head like the other noises around me. I'm listening, but not to her.

As we leave, I detect the rumble of a diesel engine. I drop my tray down fast on the nearest counter and run to the door and outside to the parking lot.

But there is no silver diesel truck with a zombie bumper sticker. It's a black truck with a bunch of kids tumbling out of it. My throat tightens. Mom touches my shoulder and says my name, but I let my hair fall over my face so she can't see my eyes are getting wet.

Back at the motel, I've thrown myself face down on the bed.

"Jeremy, what were you doing there all day?"

I mumble that I don't know. But I do know. I just don't want to say it. It's kind of a secret, what I did at the tree house. It's not the first time I've been there and sat in the tunnel and played the game.

It's just the first time I've done it without my dad there.

CHAPTER 3

GUY TIME

On the occasional Saturday, Dad tells Mom we are going to have some "guy time." Then we go to Dave's Burger Joint. Dad gets me a vanilla milkshake and himself an iced coffee and sits at the tables by the tree house while I play the game with the little kids. I know I am too old for the tree house, but that's where Dad always wants to go for guy time, so I made up the game so I wouldn't be bored.

Sometimes I looked down from my perch and Dad was gone but he always came back. Sometimes I would see this other man sitting there with him, and this other man had a little kid. That guy's kid was not fun. He was loud and cried at everything. He was chubby and dirty, and he did not like the game, so I left him alone. Except for the time he stopped and poked me on the arm, and I looked at him through my hair.

The chubby kid pointed down to the table and asked, "Is that your dad?"

I answered by rolling my eyes up and down.

"My dad said your dad owes him money."

I shrugged, and the chubby kid stuck out his tongue and waddled away. A few minutes later they left, and my dad called up to me that it was time to go even though I hadn't finished my vanilla milkshake. We never saw that kid and his dad there again.

That was the last guy time we had.

Mom says we are going to have a *fresh start*. Everything we had is gone so let's just pretend none of this happened and have a do-over. We shop for things at GetMor4Less which is weird because Mom hates that store. When we get to the checkout, she pulls out a GetMor4Less gift card.

I don't like the fresh start stuff. I like my old stuff. I like my old room. The apartment Mom rented has furniture that isn't anything like our real furniture. The sofa is orange and scratchy, and I hate orange so I won't be sitting on that. Which is fine because I prefer the floor anyway. There is an old analog TV, the big kind that is like a heavy box and you need two strong people to lift it. My bedroom has a bunk bed. That's okay. My room also has a balcony with a big tree right next to it. Roof access.

"Eventually we will get better furniture. Just the basics for now." I watch her put groceries away in the pantry. She places a bag of peanut butter sandwich cookies on the table for me. I'm glad those made the "basics" list.

"Hey, Jeremy, I need to talk to you about something."

I knew it. She's going to tell me something I don't want to hear. The cookies are meant to calm me.

I don't want to eat a peanut butter sandwich cookie right now because if what she says it isn't good news and I eat the cookies, they will be ruined forever. And I don't want to lose them. Mom doesn't understand this. She pushes the package toward me.

"Jeremy, I got the fire investigator's report today. It said the fire started in your room. Is there anything you want to tell me?"

Is she crazy? Of course, I *should* tell her, but I don't *want* to. She's asking the wrong question. What she should say to me is, "Jeremy, what did you learn by starting a fire using a 9-volt battery and a wad of steel wool?" Now, that's a good question.

"This has been really hard, I know. And I also know whatever happened was an accident, but we still have to talk about it."

A couple years ago, I stopped cutting my hair. No bribes or pleading would get me to cut it. It eventually grew so that it completely covers my eyes down to my chin. When I don't want to talk about something, I let it fall so that no one can see my eyes. It's like drawing a curtain across my face. Bow, applause, curtain, exit stage. See ya.

I give Mom my best *wall of hair* stare.

"It *was* an accident, wasn't it?"

"I'm sorry." I drop my head until my chin almost touches my chest. House is gone. Stuff is gone. Dad is gone. It wasn't an accident. It wasn't on purpose. It is another thing on the long list of things I have ruined by being me.

"When is Dad coming home?" She doesn't answer for over twenty heartbeats.

"I'm sorry, Jeremy. We are getting a divorce."

Goodbye, peanut butter sandwich cookies. It doesn't matter that I didn't eat them. I get up from the table and go to my room and climb up to the top bunk. I curl up with my knees to my chest and press my head against the rail of the bunk bed until I hear the creak of the wood straining, like a bending tree branch.

I stay that way until the room begins to darken. Mom comes in to check on me a few times, and I pretend to be asleep. I hear her turn on the TV and turn it off a few minutes later. She probably realized it useless without a DVR player. I climb down from the bunk and check that she's gone to bed.

I go outside on my balcony and study the tree that grows just a couple feet from the building. I pull myself up onto the balcony railing and hold onto a tree branch to inspect the roof. It's not as easy as climbing out my bedroom window directly onto the roof. If I climb another branch higher into the tree, I'm close enough to jump from the tree onto the roof.

It's steeper than my old roof. I stretch out on my back with my face to the darkening sky and watch the stars come into focus. From my shirt pocket, I take out the book of hotel matches and feel all twenty red phosphorous tipped cardboard sticks.

Whenever I look at the night sky from the rooftop, something happens. I am a safe distance from everything that might mess with me, and I can see all around. The stars each light up their little piece of the sky. Between them, I imagine faint lines connecting each star. I connect the dots across the sky like I am solving a puzzle. Questions bubble up in my head.

What made the stars? *Exploding gasses inside a nebula.*

How far away are they? *On a good night, you can see* 19,000,000,000,000,000 *miles.*

How many zeroes was that? *Fifteen zeroes make a quadrillion.*

Which burns faster, a house or a forest? *A house fire will double in size every minute.*

If I fall off the roof, will I die? *Do you want to die?*

What did I learn by starting a fire using a 9-volt battery and a wad of steel wool?

How to make everything you love disappear.

Chapter 4

Code Talkers

A woman visits my mom and brings bags clothes and a GetMor4Less gift card. She brings a box of games for me. I sift through the box hoping to find a laptop or something I can take apart, like an old tablet. There is Hi Ho Cherry-O. Chutes and Ladders. Memory. A 1000-piece picture puzzle of a castle on a green, foggy hillside somewhere that is obviously not Arizona. A few kids' movies on DVDs. She also brought a DVD player. It has a sticker on it that says $5.00.

Mom gives it to me and whispers, "That is not for you to disassemble."

I want to ask the woman for tools next time or even some interesting rocks. But Mom nudges me, so I mumble thank you and take the box to the living room.

My laptop was obliterated in the fire. I miss playing Minecraft. I don't dare mention anything about that to Mom. She thinks games are a big waste of time. To me, it's one of the few things that make sense.

Almost everything in Minecraft is a three-dimensional block. Soil, minerals, wood, stone, iron ore, gold ore, diamond ore, and ice are all blocks. Even things that should be plump and round are square, like a pumpkin or a woolly sheep. I build houses, forts, roads, and villages, then destroy and build them again. I raise animals and use them for materials and food. Cows become beef and leather. Sheep become mutton or wool. Not just any wool but a whole spectrum of colors. Of course, there are monsters. Skeletons, Creepers, and Zombies are a few of my favorites. Most monsters are fierce and destructive. You fight them with swords you make yourself. You must always be working out your defenses because Skeletons are precise with their arrows. Creepers explode causing destruction all around them. Zombies attack at night, but in the daylight, they burst into flames. The best thing about Minecraft is that you don't win at Minecraft. You accumulate. You hunt and build and buy and sell and trade and fight. I build my own world where I know what to say and do. Me. I actually know things.

The woman sits at the kitchen table with my mom while I set up the DVD player. She says words to my mom that are meant to hide what they are talking about. Mom never says mean things to me, or about me, not intentionally anyway. She says cryptic things that make me feel dumb. Maybe I'm a little bit lazy today, that's something she would say. Or, maybe what I did was careless. That's one I've been thinking about a lot.

I've overheard her on her phone talking about me, in code that means something isn't right with Jeremy. Today, I hear a whole new bunch of code words.

"Accident." This is what they are calling the fire, even though I don't agree.

"Survivors." That's what the woman calls us, so I won't think it is my fault.

"Support." The box of baby games the woman brought and the GetMor4Less gift cards.

"The child." Me. Seriously.

"Support group." Circle time for grown-ups.

"Fresh start." We've already covered this one.

I insert Alice in Wonderland into the DVD player and push play even though I have no intention of watching it. It's cover so I can listen without looking like I am listening.

When the woman leaves, Mom says she is going to GetMor4Less for a few things and asks me to stay by myself for a bit. I ask how long and she sighs.

"An hour, maybe?"

"Okay." I pretend to be falling asleep on the floor. When she is gone, I jump up and get to work. I have an hour, maybe.

I look through papers on the kitchen counter and her bedside table for any clue about what is going to happen next. I hate surprises. Even good ones. A surprise means that something I am not expecting—therefore not ready to handle—is about to happen. I go mute. I freeze like an ice block. You could hand me a million dollars and ask me if I was happy and I would not even say thanks.

I find what I'm looking for. The Folder of Failure. The story of my life in one plain beige, boring folder. Inside are the bad things about me. I am still looking for the Folder of Good Things, but I think Mom doesn't have one.

Leafing through the Folder of Failure, I put aside the old things and inspect new questionnaires Mom has filled out.

Am I depressed? Distracted? Violent?

Depressed? Distracted? Mom answered "always" to both.

Violent? I burned down my house. Was that violent? It hurt everyone, so it must have been. But, she filled in the bubble for "never" next to violent. Mom always pretends things are better than they really are.

For Gets in trouble at school, she filled in "often." I must argue with this question because they don't define "trouble." Is failing a test trouble? Or is threatening to bite someone trouble? Two very different kinds of trouble. It's hard to move on after this. There are so many questions it makes me dizzy to look at them. I put the questionnaires back in the folder. All of this means something that I don't want to be true. Something Mom hasn't said out loud yet but might as well be painted on the walls.

I know what all this means. I just don't have words for it.

CHAPTER 5

SOMETHING OTHER THAN DREAD

It's not too hard to puzzle out that when summer vacation ends, I will be going to a new school.

It doesn't fill me with dread, though, the idea of a new school. I don't know what to call it. It's part excited to go somewhere new because maybe it will be better, and part sad because all evidence points to the conclusion it will be a disappointment. Imagine you are being told you are going to ride a roller coaster, but when you get there, it's just an old storefront with a stupid horsey ride that takes a quarter to go in a circle. And you are expected to love every nanosecond of it and ignore the fact that you were lied to.

Every time I go to a new school, it's not bad in the beginning. Lots of attention from teachers. A nice kid is assigned to show me around. I get invited to his birthday party. I get a good grade on a math test. It's all great.

That lasts for a couple of weeks before it starts to fall apart. The nice kid eats lunch with some other kids. Now I don't want to go to his birthday party because he obviously doesn't like me and his mom probably made him invite me. So, I throw away the invitation before Mom sees it.

Every day, I brace myself, stomach churning as I walk into the classroom. Everyone will look at me and think, *idiot new kid.* I am lost from the moment I sit down, thus proving their insults true. I try to pay attention, but everything happens too fast. Next thing you know I'm ditching class and hiding out in the bathroom. *Idiot new kid.*

After school, I play Minecraft, but I look like I'm doing my homework. I fall asleep and forget to do my homework. Even when Mom asks me if homework is done, I lie and say yes. Or, I do my homework, but I forget to turn it in. I try to study for tests, but I fall asleep five minutes into studying. History is the worst. I can't get through one stupid paragraph of the reading because it is so stinking boring. I almost never do the reading assignments in English, either. I stare at words for hours, but they don't imprint on my brain. Then I fail.

When the calls from school start, Mom gets the sad and worried look. She asks about homework every single day. She wants to see it. I know she'll get mad that it's not done so I tell her I don't have any or I finished it in class. I know that I am buying time until the grade reports come out. If she misses the email that says grades were sent home, I've got one more week before parent-teacher conferences. I lose the paper that tells her it is time for parent-teacher conferences to buy more time.

Eventually, Mom learns that I don't do my homework. I don't turn in my assignments. I do surprisingly well on science tests, but I'm failing because I don't write the lab reports. Every teacher says I am smart, but my problem is *I don't care*. Plus, *I'm lazy*.

Things start to fall apart. Mom unravels my string of lies. She says the code word *this isn't the right school for you* when what she really means is *time to move on to the next disappointing ride*.

Only one teacher was ever on my side. Preschool. Miss Emily. Miss Emily was my favorite because when it was time to sit and be quiet—also known as circle time—she would pull out a piece of paper and fold it. From my X in the circle, I would scoot closer to her because I knew that paper thing was for me. I scooted to Miss Emily even at the risk of Miss Pat scolding me or grabbing my arm and dragging me back to my X. Miss Pat always seated me as far away from Miss Emily as the earth is to the sun. Ninety-three million miles.

If Minecraft was preschool, Miss Pat was a Skeleton. Not just any Skeleton. A Wither. A floating, three-headed, ghost that attacks by shooting skulls at you. A Wither doesn't just attack you, it slowly drains your health away. It turns all your hearts to black.

But Miss Emily, she was a wolf: a companion. A Wolf keeps you safe and drives away monsters. When circle time was over, Miss Emily would slip me the paper crane, and it went right in my pocket with all the other things I'd collected that day, hiding it before Miss Pat saw and took it away. Miss Emily made me forty-seven paper cranes in all. Miss Pat took all but the ten I hid inside my socks.

Every morning I watched the door for Miss Emily to arrive. She looked like a valentine in a red sweater with white hearts that she always wore in the classroom. Then one day she was gone. I waited every day for her to come back.

I avoided Miss Pat who hollered at me to sit on my X and *be still*. What did that even mean? Be still? I would get up and run away and hide in the supply closet or under the art table. Miss Pat would find me because my wiggling toes that could not *be still* inside my shoes gave me away. She'd yank me out by my arm and squeeze until it hurt. Once, she grabbed my jaw between her rough Wither skeleton fingers and pinched while she hissed in her lava voice that crept and scalded me with words I did understand.

You are a terrible boy.

She'd write my mom a note with those words, always on bright orange, *you're in trouble* paper, never folded, but placed face down in my cubby, so everyone knew I got a note home. I hated the trouble notes. I hated the look on Mom's face when she saw the note in my cubby. Miss Emily never gave me that *not again* look.

I hated orange because it was the color of trouble. I couldn't eat orange food. Orange made me angry. With Miss Emily gone, red made me sad, so I couldn't talk to anyone wearing red. I wouldn't touch anything red or use a red crayon.

After Mom showed me what happens when you wash socks that have paper cranes hidden inside them, she got me an origami book and a stack of colored square papers. I promptly removed all the orange and red ones and flushed them. Then I followed the picture guides and made my own cranes. I loved how they came out perfect and pointy when I followed the picture guides. I slowly made every crease with my fingernail across the papers until the edges were sharp like arrow points. I made more cranes. Then owls and bats. Frogs. Pigs. Hearts. Rhinos. Every sea creature imaginable. Yoda. Ninja stars. Every kind of star.

But Miss Pat didn't like my fingers moving, even when paper folding kept the rest of me still. Miss Pat insisted that every part of me be still. I said that it was impossible. I said that my lungs were still filling with air and my heart was pumping blood. Miss Pat put tape over my mouth and put me in time out for the day.

Because Miss Emily was gone, I drowned in a sea of orange trouble.

CHAPTER 6

THE FOLDER OF FAILURE

Mom tells me about the new school in the morning. This time there are powdered sugar donuts on the table. I look at her, look at the donuts and sigh loudly. Then I drop my head on the table and bang it, just a little.

Tomorrow we'll go visit the school. Today we see a doctor who will talk to me about things I don't want to talk about.

No. My dad will not be there.

Mom doesn't use the word test. She uses the code word evaluation. Instead of going to the doctor to be measured and probed and stuck with needles and not allowed to handle any of the tools for more than a second or two, I will be asked a gazillion questions about my least favorite topics. I know this because when we get ready to leave, Mom brings all the questionnaires she has stuffed into the Folder of Failure.

The folder is fatter with new papers. It only comes out into view when we go to a doctor, or I'm sent to the vice principal's office for falling asleep in class or for saying true things that other people don't believe. She keeps the folder at her office, so I rarely get to sneak a look at it. But I can see the orange trouble notes from preschool. Blue slips from the school office, year after year of them. I hate this folder. It's full of mistakes and just seeing it makes me want to throw up. I want to hurl it out the car window as we drive. Why did everything else about me burn up but not the folder?

We pull into an office building with huge trees whose branches jut out over the parking spaces to make shady spots. We park under a perfect climbing tree, and I consider ditching the doctor's office and getting myself up to the very highest branch of that tree where no one can reach me. Mom already knows what I'm thinking.

"Let's go, Jeremy. No tree climbing today."

The office lobby is filled with small tables, kiddie chairs and toys, blocks, books, crayons and lots of paper. No television. No video games. It's quiet. I can hear the tree branches sway outside in the wind. A woman emerges from a hallway and reaches out a hand to Mom, then to me.

"Hi, Jeremy. I'm Dr. Nugent."

I keep my hands in my pockets. Today I have added a rock with sharp edges that I found on the apartment playground. I swap out the stuff in my pockets because after a while my fingers get bored and need something new. Mom nudges me to shake Dr. Nugent's. I don't like shaking hands. Why is the first thing you are expected to do when you meet someone new is touch them? I keep my hand in my pocket and hold onto the rock.

"A hello is just fine, Jeremy."

I mumble hello.

Mom hands the Folder of Failure to Dr. Nugent.

"It's all in there."

She says goodbye and Dr. Nugent leads me down the hallway to a room and motions for me to sit in a chair next to her desk.

"Do you remember me at all?" She asks.

So far, I've only really looked at her shoes. They are very plain shoes, almost the same color as the grayish carpet. They are sandals like my mom wears. What gets my attention isn't that, but her toenails. They have rainbow decals on them. ROYGBV.

I shake my head.

"That's okay, you were little last time I saw you."

From a desk drawer, she pulls out a square piece of sky blue colored paper. I watch her fingers make the first two folds, corners to opposite corners. I watch it take the shape I know. She places it on the desk.

At first, I feel dizzy. I take in a deep breath, and I blow it out, loudly.

"Miss Emily?"

She smiles and nods. She gets me a drink of water.

"Is this okay with you, Jeremy?"

I don't answer. The paper crane looks just like I remember them; the pointy wing tips are crisp, not soft and torn like the cranes I carried home in my socks. Even though I have not made one for years, I remember how to make a paper crane. At each step, it takes on a different geometric shape. Rectangle. Isosceles triangle. Square. Then it becomes three dimensional. Then it has wings, and a head and a bill. And sometimes the wings are movable.

"You left. Why did you leave?"

"You don't remember?"

I search for a memory I do not have. Miss Emily is a blur of red and white in my head, a set of hands making paper birds. A smudge of rainbow-colored toenail. A Valentine I might have saved because it was different than the others but I couldn't remember who gave it to me. I trace the jagged points of the rock in my pocket, feeling stupid.

"It was my student teaching post. When the semester ended, it was time for me to go back to school. We had a going away party, and you gave me a robin eggshell you found in the play yard."

"I did?"

"Yes! We couldn't keep you out of the tree. You were always climbing. You knew exactly where the eggshell came from and you wanted to see that baby bird."

This makes me smile a little. But then I remember the rest. I remember Miss Pat pulling me down by the belt and shaking me up against the tree trunk while she scolded me in front of the others. I held the bird egg cautiously in my hand, trying not to crush it.

Miss Emily interrupts my remembering to ask, "Do you know why you are here?"

I fidget with the rock. I can't look at her face. I know why I am here, but I don't want to say those words.

Chapter 7

Never Sometimes Often

Miss Emily asks me lots of questions. It's the first time anyone has asked me questions like this without my mom in the room, and at first, I can't even open my mouth to speak. It takes me a long time to answer and I half-expect Mom to jump in. I glance at Miss Emily to see if she is getting impatient. Her face doesn't change. She looks through the Folder of Failure, including the questionnaires that Mom brought, but she never tells me to hurry up.

Miss Emily asks about school. Do I have difficulty paying attention? Did it affect my school work? Do I forget what I am supposed to do? Has this ever gotten me into trouble?

Give examples.

Yes. Yes. Yes. And yes. Those are the answers Mom would give. I tell Miss Emily she is holding the folder full of examples.

She slides a paper in front of me and sets a pencil down on top of it.

"I'm going to step out for a few minutes while you fill out this questionnaire."

I hate forms, especially the bubble answer type. You must choose from the answers provided, but they are never the right answers. Not any of them. How can I answer the question when the answer depends on information I don't have?

On Miss Emily's form, the only answers allowed are NEVER, SOMETIMES, OFTEN or VERY OFTEN.

On a regular day, I have trouble making choices, but this is worse. An answer can be sort of right but there is more I need to say about it, and that's not allowed. Then I get thinking about some other question that is five skips ahead. Before I decide what answer is the closest to what I would say if they'd just let me say it, I lose my place and don't answer anything. This process takes a millennium.

I decide to do it the way I want to do it because it's Miss Emily, who never gets angry.

"I forget things that I have learned." I check VERY OFTEN, then write in the margin: "Not regarding food or Minecraft. I hate onions, and I had to learn that only once."

"I don't like schoolwork where I have to think a lot." VERY OFTEN. I write: "This is the stupidest question ever. I never STOP thinking. Thinking isn't the problem, it's that my brain is thinking about everything, like every voice in the world is telling me what to do all at once."

"I make careless mistakes or have trouble paying close attention to details." VERY OFTEN. I write: "This is inaccurate because there isn't an answer for ALWAYS."

Miss Emily walks back into the room with another test

booklet.

"How's it going, Jeremy?" She looks over the page I am working on and sees that I answered three questions and did a lot of writing.

"Let's give this one a shot, instead."

I groan and ask for a bathroom break.

"Just five minutes," she says. "How about this. I'll ask you the questions, and you mark the answer on the sheet."

Miss Emily reads the first question and the multiple-choice answers and right away I know I am going to fail this one, too. This is a test to figure out if I would like to kill myself.

"I don't need this test," I say. "I would not like to kill myself."

Miss Emily writes something down. "That's a relief, but this test is about feelings. I know that feelings are hard to put into words, so I want you to choose a response that most closely describes your feelings."

I take in a deep breath and then blow it out.

"Fine."

A. Nothing will ever work out for me.

B. I am not sure if things will work out for me.

C. Things will work out okay for me.

"Does anyone ever answer that question the same way two days in a row? Why isn't there a choice for sometimes I think I'm okay and other times I think I'm going to get mobbed in my sleep by cave spiders?"

"Tell me which answer most closely describes how you feel."

"C, because I know how to defeat cave spiders."

Miss Emily puts the test booklet aside.

"Jeremy, can you tell me in your own words why you are here?"

I groan and bang my forehead on the desk. "Please, can we just stop?"

"Okay. Is there something else you'd like to do right now?"

I lift my head and look out the window. "I'd like to climb a tree."

It's monsoon season in Phoenix. The sun is darkened by a whole sky of swirling gray clouds. Miss Emily stands next to the mesquite tree. The wind blows her hair around, and she doesn't once tell me to hurry up, even though the rain could come at any second. I seat myself on a branch. I have a lot of tree climbing experience. I also have a lot of sitting and watching experience.

A wall of wind and dust whip parking lot debris into cyclones. But Miss Emily doesn't tell me to get down. She lifts her hands to catch the hair that flies wildly around her face. Her skirt and blouse billow and flatten, then billow again, but she doesn't move from where she is standing even when dark wet splotches appear on the tarry parking lot surface. Lightning threatens between the gusts of wind.

The tree creaks while I watch leaves and trash skitter on the ground and crash into car tires. An empty soda can clanks by. Another lightning bolt flashes. I remember how the electricity from the 9V battery lit up the fine steel wool fibers in a surge of yellow liquid-like lava. Racing through every twisty fiber and sparking. It was mesmerizing. It was an experiment. I made mistakes. I used cotton balls to make more fire. I got scared when I heard Dad on the stairs, and I covered it with a piece of paper. I can't call it an accident. I don't know what to call it.

"Are you ready to go back inside?" Miss Emily calls. I swing down, and we walk fast to get out of the rain.

"Jeremy? Are you able to answer that question now?"

"Which question?" I mumble.

"Why do you think you are here?"

Big breath in. Big breath out. Miss Emily must have forgotten all those years ago, that the egg fell from my hand and broke on the sidewalk and I screamed at Miss Pat. I had words then, and they were STOP! YOU ARE HURTING IT!

But Miss Pat's bony claws shaking me until I dropped it? Taping my mouth shut so I couldn't even say the truth? I have words for that. These words come easily. These are the words I tell Miss Emily. The only words that explain everything. Miss Pat's words.

I am a terrible boy.

CHAPTER 8

UNSTEADY GROUND

I'm not ready, and we're late. This could apply to any day.

It's time to leave, and Mom is hollering from the kitchen. She doesn't have to yell because the apartment is small so I can hear her just fine, but she is used to yelling at me to hurry up. I am used to ignoring her. When she opens my door, I'm looking for my left flip-flop.

"We have an appointment, Jeremy, remember?"

Sometimes I don't remember. Today, I just don't want to go. I'm not excited about seeing the new school. I'm apprehensive. That word I learned from Miss Emily yesterday. It means I'm not quite ready for something. It means worried with a little bit of scared mixed in. We discussed this while we walked back to her office after I climbed down from the mesquite tree.

Miss Emily asked me about the fire, which I said was not on purpose and was also not an accident. She asked about my dad. I was apprehensive about both of those things. Today, I am apprehensive about another evaluation.

Mom brings the Folder of Failure into the new school which is called Equator School. I see the detested orange notes. There's absolutely nothing in this room but a black conference table and black chairs and a copy machine. There is nothing to look at, nothing to do. I might as well be wearing pants made of pine needles. I think about climbing the tree at Miss Emily's office while the monsoon storm rolled in over us, only I imagine it swinging me back and forth until I lose my balance on the branch. I imagine hitting every branch of the tree on the way down until I am falling, headfirst, into the pavement. That would be better than this.

Mom shuffles her papers and checks her watch. She reaches to move my hair from my face, and I jerk back. She knows I hate her touching my hair.

"Move it out of your eyes, please." I give my head a toss to satisfy her. Finally, there's a knock on the door, and a man walks in.

Mom stands up and introduces herself, then shakes his hand.

"Craig. A pleasure to meet you." He's a skinny guy with reddish-orange hair and freckles.

"Nice to meet you, Jeremy. You can call me Tully." He does not offer a handshake. Curious.

"You said your name is Craig."

"Tully is my last name. The students call me Tully."

Mom dives right into her usual speech. I'm not a bad kid. I'm distracted and depressed. I have difficulty staying on task in class and relating to my peers. I notice she does not mention the fire. Tully nods. She says we're here for a fresh start. He passes her some papers to read and sign.

I dig my hands into both my pockets and begin counting how many ripples there are on the circumference of a bottle cap (twenty-two). Tully skims the Folder of Failure, then makes a copy of it. I'm trying to disappear when Tully slides something across the table to me.

"Jeremy, here you go." It's a Rubik's cube. "Fix that for me."

I look it over. I make a couple twists and stop.

"I have a question."

"Go ahead."

"If everyone on Earth jumped up at exactly same time, what would happen?"

He doesn't miss a beat. "Essentially, nothing. Seven billion humans are no match for something that weighs six sextillion tons. Hey, that's a great idea for an experiment."

Mom looks confused. She doesn't get what just happened. Then she smiles and turns back to Tully.

"I'd really like him to pay attention to this conversation," she says, in her I am polite but annoyed voice.

Tully, my new favorite person, says, "Now, he will."

I carry the Rubik's Cube on our tour of the school. It appears like any other school at first. Everything looks brand new because it's been cleaned up over the summer. The long hallways have gleaming floors not yet grimed up by shoe marks. Shiny black lockers line the walls. Doors to classrooms have little glass windows to peek in and see how late you are and if you can slip in without being seen. We step into a classroom while Tully explains how this isn't just any classroom. In the corner of the room is an area called Distraction Station. There is a sofa and chairs and bins full of stuff like I keep in my pockets. Scrabble tiles and dice. Doorknobs. Magnets. The insides of watches and clocks. Screwdrivers every size. Lots and lots of Legos. Also, circuits, strips of cloth, yarn, knitting needles, jigsaw puzzles, and bottle caps.

Next is the cafeteria. As of this morning, this is important to Mom because she read that food makes me more distracted, and she threw out everything that has food coloring, sugar, and flour. I'm now gluten-free, which means that I am hungry all the time. Tully explains that the cafeteria only serves food that is made fresh every morning and doesn't have any of that bad stuff. Every kid gets to pick from a menu or bring their lunch from home. He lists the stuff that isn't allowed in the cafeteria: no peanuts, sugar, flour, food coloring. I remind Mom that I don't like carrots or Brussels sprouts.

Tully leans in and says, "I don't like Brussels sprouts, either. But the carrots here are phenomenal."

Phenomenal carrots are still orange, I think.

After the cafeteria, Tully shows us the outside playground which looks like any other playground with picnic tables and a grassy field.

"Notice anything unusual?" Tully asks. Mom takes a breath to speak, but Tully quickly stops her. "Sorry, I was asking Jeremy. See if you can spot more than one unusual thing."

I'm looking, but I don't see anything unexpected. Tully tells me to go ahead and walk around like I'm on an Easter egg hunt except I'm not sure what I'm looking for. I see tetherball, a basketball court, a volleyball net and a sand pit. It's a pretty big playground for a small school. Then I see it: a rock climbing wall. Right up to the side of the building. Unusual? Maybe. But when I point at it I can tell Tully wasn't talking about that. Then I look down at my feet and notice I am standing on a chessboard. An enormous life-size chess board.

"It's true," Tully says. "Recess here gets pretty wild."

Even I have to laugh at that. Then he shows me the playing pieces, which are hidden behind a storage wall. They are statues made of foam.

At the end of the tour, Tully walks us through the front lobby and says he's looking forward to seeing me in class next week. I hand him the Rubik's Cube, which I haven't even come close to solving.

"You can bring it to school with you if you'd like."

Now I'm convinced. This can't be a real school. It must be a trick.

✻

Next, we go to a doctor. Again, with the grades and the list of my problems. Again, with the Folder of Failure. The doctor asks me questions, but Mom jumps in because I take too long to answer.

"So, you have a hard time doing homework?" the doctor asks. "What's hard about it?"

Mom's foot jiggles impatiently. I look at the floor and Mom can't stand it anymore.

"He tries but he falls asleep, or I find him just sitting there staring at his computer or playing games."

"I don't have a computer anymore," I clarify.

The doctor doesn't ask or care about the computer. I get stuck on the next questions. Why am I failing school? Is it too hard or too boring? Do I get in trouble in class? What do I like to do when I'm not in school? Do I have friends? Do I have an appetite?

He looks into my ears and nose and eyes, listens to my heart and then we are done. As we leave, the nurse hands something to Mom.

"Once a day with food, and we'll see him back in two weeks."

On the way home, I fall asleep in the car. When we get home, Mom shakes me awake, and for a moment I can't remember where I am. I vaguely recall the Rubik's Cube and the new school with the chessboard and rock wall on the playground. But climbing the stairs back to the apartment makes me remember where I am.

Fresh start. New home. New school. New stuff. Dad is gone. The world I knew has been deleted, and I have no choice but to re-spawn. No matter how much Mom tries to make it sound like the best thing that ever happened to us, my life is locked into Survival Mode.

CHAPTER 9

WHY CIRCLES

Breakfast doesn't go down. I move the scrambled eggs around on the plate and stack the square cut potatoes in a tower and knock it down again with my fork. Mom gives me the five-minute warning. I am now taking meds. Meds is Mom's word as in "These meds should help you focus and feel better." The little blue pill I swallow leaves a bitter taste on my tongue. I try to wash it away with milk but that tastes worse. I scrape my food into the trash and use the dishtowel to scrub the bitter spot from my tongue.

For the first day of school, I have a new backpack (black), a lunch box that has three zippered compartments on the outside and a carabiner attaching it to my backpack. In the side pocket is a water bottle with a sports top (BPA free, whatever that means, but Mom thought it was important). My new sneakers have double-knotted laces because I don't like the feel of hook and loop fasteners. I prefer my socks with no seams (also black), a royal blue shirt with breast pocket and black athletic shorts with pockets, both with no tags. My backpack is heavy with three-ring binders, loose-leaf college-ruled paper, mechanical pencils with 7mm lead, and a plain white eraser with a zombie face on it that I drew with a ballpoint pen. Stuffed in the other side pocket is the Rubik's Cube, which I have not yet solved.

When we get to school, I want to throw up. I let my hair fall over my eyes as I get out of the car and sling the pack over my shoulder. Tully is holding open the door and greeting everyone as they walk in.

"Good morning, Jeremy!" I hear when I walk through the door. "Everyone to the MPR, that's the multi-purpose room."

I follow the crowd since I have no idea where the MPR is. It turns out to be the cafeteria. I stand in a line to get a first-day packet at a table staffed by two upper-grade students. Inside the MPR, kids are sitting at tables talking with each other. A few are playing board games. Some are outside jumping on the trampoline or playing tetherball or just standing around. Whatever I thought was different about Equator School is lost now. I take a seat in the very back as close to the exit door as I can get but still have a full view of the room. I close the curtain of hair over my eyes. I wish I could remember where the bathroom is.

My fingers find the jagged rock in my pocket, but today it doesn't help at all. Not even the bottle cap feels right. I open the large white envelope that has my name printed on it and take out a name tag. It says my name, Grade 7, and a symbol "Ru" on it with the number 44. I search my head for the name of the element RU, but I can't find it. Then I hear a voice I know. It comes from behind me.

"Hi, Jeremy." I turn my head and move my hair to see Miss Emily standing there. Before I can respond, a girl, holding a little boy's hand, calls out.

"Good morning, Dr. Nugent."

"Good morning, Bree. Welcome back. Good morning to you, Jeremy," Miss Emily says to the little boy.

The girl looks at me and says, "Hey, a new kid."

There's something in her voice that makes me sit up straight, possibly by surprise. She's almost as tall as Miss Emily, who isn't very tall. I nod at the girl, who studies me with that look Mom gets when she is about to tell me to do something I don't want to do.

"Hi, Dr. Nugent." It is hard to call her that.

"Why don't you come closer to the front, so you can hear the presentation? I'll introduce you to some kids I know."

It's hard to say no to her. I pick up my backpack and the first-day packet, even though I don't want to sit closer to the front and I don't want to meet new kids. I follow Dr. Nugent to a table near the front of the room where several boys are playing a game with dice.

"Good morning," she says. All three of them look up and smile at her and say hello.

"This is Jeremy. Jeremy meet Ben, David, and Trace. You are all in Ruthenium element. Can you boys make sure Jeremy finds his way today?"

"Sure," they answer. I notice how everyone snaps to attention when she talks.

"Have a great first day," she says and walks to the platform at the front of the room, where Tully is testing out a microphone.

"All right, settle in and let's get rolling." He says "settle in" and not "settle down" or "be still."

I notice that fuzzy pipe cleaners in the school colors, purple and white, are heaped on the tables like pick-up sticks. No one has touched them yet. Tully introduces the people on the platform, and when he does, the kid named Trace reaches over and picks up a purple and a white and twists them into a mustache shape. He holds it to his face and winks. Ben and David laugh.

Tully introduces Dr. Emily Nugent, the school psychologist, and three teachers on the platform. I forget their names as soon as I hear them. Now Trace makes something that looks like a gear. Then I notice a few other kids have picked up pipe cleaners and are making shapes out of them. My own hands are in my pockets when Ben leans over.

"You want some?" He offers me a couple of the pipe cleaners.

"What are they for?"

"Fidgets," he says. I take the pipe cleaners and hold them in my lap.

Tully calls out the names of elements on the periodic table, and as he does, kids raise their hands if they are part of that group. Other element names like Argon, Copper, and Oxygen are called out.

A few seats away I see Bree sitting next to the little Jeremy. She doesn't touch the pipe cleaners in front of her. Instead, her hands are folded, and her eyes are looking straight down the table at me. I look away and hide behind my hair. She also raises her hand when Ruthenium is called.

The room never goes silent when Tully talks. Instead, there is a low murmur and the swishy sound of hands moving around on the table tops. Tully doesn't rap on the podium or scold anyone. He asks a question.

"If you are returning to Equator School, please stand up."

Two-thirds of the room stand up, including Trace, Ben, David, and Bree.

"Welcome back!" He says enthusiastically. "Those of you still seated, meet your trail guides. You'll find that things work a little differently at Equator School than wherever you came from. Every student standing is expected to help you find your way, so look to them for assistance. Their name tags are marked with a purple star so you can recognize them."

Trace, Ben, and David all have purple stars. Bree has a purple star.

"There is a science to the way we place you in these groups, so no switching. Your class schedule is in your white packet along with your locker number and combination. Also in your packet is a blank sheet of paper and a pencil. Please take those out now and write your name on the top, then draw a circle the approximate circumference of a soda can." On a whiteboard, he draws a circle.

"Inside the circle, please write the answer to this question." In black marker on a whiteboard, he writes: Why are you here?

Miss Emily's question. Does everyone have to answer it before they can come here? The purple stars are writing already. They know a secret the new kids don't. Trace is done in about one minute. Ben and David finish and resume their dice game. I leave my circle blank. No way am I putting it down on paper so everyone can see. I don't want to read it out loud if I get called on.

Tully says, "If you wrote an answer to the question, raise your hand."

Mostly only purple stars raise their hands.

"Those of you who left it blank did it for one of two reasons. Either you aren't sure, or you don't want anyone else to know. Now, I'm going to tell you why I am here."

Tully writes one word in his circle on the whiteboard: Truth.

"Truth. What is truth? It's the real thing. It's the real you, the real me, the secrets we keep from everyone about what goes on inside our heads. At this school, you are not the weird kid. You are not left behind, pushed away, or punished for being unable to sit in a chair. At this school, you will discover your gifts. You will discover your purpose. There are no handicaps. There are no consequences for being different."

When Tully says the word "consequences", he puts finger quotes in the air. Some kids laugh.

"I am here to help you discover your own truth. The truth that you will eventually write down inside that empty circle.

"I promise every one of you, that before the end of your first year at Equator, you'll know exactly why you are here. The real why, not the why that makes you confused or ashamed."

The purple stars applaud. Except for Bree. She just sits there, looking sideways at me.

CHAPTER 10

SUPERPOWERS

When Tully dismisses us for our first class of the day, everyone passes their papers, face down, to the end of the table where Dr. Nugent picks them up. I don't. I fold up the paper with the empty circle and stuff it in my backpack. Some kids are more dramatic. They crumple it up and throw it on the floor or in the trash. One girl has folded hers into a triangle and flicks it across the table. Some didn't even draw the circle on the paper. But all the purple stars drew circles. Ben pulled out a compass from his backpack to draw a perfect circle. Compared to Ben's circle, mine was a flop. Egg-shaped and uneven.

I don't know what else to do so I follow Trace, Ben, and David out of the MPR into the hallway. They have a swagger like kids do when they know each other, and they aren't the new kid anymore.

"Flying," says Trace.

"Rock-crushing," Ben says.

"That's two words," responds David.

"It's hyphenated," Ben argues. They discuss if hyphenated words are one word or two and do not agree. Then Trace turns around and points at me.

"What's your superpower? One word. Go."

I don't know why but it is the first thing that comes to mind.

"Falling?"

Trace smiles. Ben and David laugh. I'm sure they are laughing because it's a stupid answer.

Then David says, "Vomiting," and they all practically collapse on the floor with laughter.

※

In every class, there is something on the desk when we get there, not a textbook. In Chemistry, we are given our own whiteboards and dry-erase markers. In Language, there are granola bars and grapes. In History, with Mr. Anderson who speaks with an Australian accent and wears a battered leather outback hat, there are rocks on the table.

"See, rock-crushing!" Ben declares, triumphant.

"What does a rock have to do with history?" Mr. Anderson's voice booms over the class and the sound of rocks clunking on the desktops. "To answer that question, let's talk about the properties of rocks. Trace," he levels a pen at Trace like a magic wand.

"Three properties of your rock."

Trace doesn't hesitate. He turns the rock in his hand and looks it over.

"Gray in color, hard to break, and smooth."

"Yes!" Mr. Anderson explodes. He points the pen at another kid who has been chipping at his rock with his mechanical pencil.

"Brittle," the kid says as a piece of it flakes off. "Layered. Black."

"Extraordinary!" He points the pen again and says, "Bree, three properties of the rock in your hand."

Bree doesn't answer right away. She waits until everyone is turned around to look at her. She turns the rock over and holds it in the palm of her hand, peering at it.

"It's not breathing, so it must be dead. Also, it doesn't speak, so it's dumb. And," she licks the rock, "it's salty."

Mr. Anderson puts his pen to his temple and says, "Delightful."

Bree lets the rock fall from her hand, and it clatters loudly on the table. Mr. Anderson doesn't even jump.

"This is History class. Those are rocks. How is history like rocks?" He holds up Trace's rock. "It's all of those things you said and more. It's different for every one of us, yet it is always there. It creates the solid surface that we stand on, influencing our every decision, even when we don't know it."

Except when it melts into lava and your own history drags you down and burns you alive, I think, trying not to notice that Bree is staring like she wants to throw her rock at me.

After History, I follow Trace, Ben, and David out to the hallway. Ben and David go in separate directions. Trace points down a hall.

"I gotta take care of something. Your next class is down that way on the left."

My schedule lists Room 3.14. The hallway is emptying fast, and Room 3.14 sounds like a joke. It must be a mistake, but Trace is already gone so I can't ask him. I am not going to ask someone else. I busy myself studying the inside of my locker, and when I look up again, I am alone.

Panic floods my brain. Now I'll be walking in with everyone staring at me. I have that shaky feeling, so I shove my pack in my locker and head into the nearby bathroom. I hunch down in a stall, my arms wrapped around my knees, waiting for the wave of nausea to pass. I take out the Rubik's Cube. My hands are busy. My mind relaxes.

I don't know how long I am like this when a pair of shoes appears outside the stall, and a girl's voice says, "Hey, new kid. You're in the wrong place."

CHAPTER 11

ROOM 3.14

Bree stomps around the boys' bathroom, muttering and kicking the paper towels on the floor.

"Boys. Are. Pigs."

I consider staying put in the stall, but she bangs on the door.

"Let's move it cube-head, it stinks in here."

I see her face peering through the open space between the door and frame. I shove the Rubik's Cube in my pack.

"How in the world did you confuse the boys' bathroom with Room 3.14?" She muses as I follow her down the hallway that wraps around the building. We come to a double door that she throws open with a flourish.

"I found one!"

I freeze, flooded again with that hot, sick feeling. Bree strides through the door like a queen entering her castle. I take a small step back, ready to retreat to the boys' bathroom again. But this is not a classroom. There are no desks and chairs. It's a gymnasium but not like any gym I've ever seen before. Tully didn't show Room 3.14 on the tour.

It's a small city inside filled with geometric shapes like pyramids and rectangles, with a circuit board of bars connecting everything together. A cement wall snakes through the center of the room, creating a maze that stops at a huge pit full of blue foam blocks the size of shoe boxes.

Bree breaks into a run toward the other side of the gym and leaps at the wall holding in the pit of foam blocks. Her fingers grasp the top edge, and her feet curl up under her knees, and she hangs there for a millisecond. She bounces up the wall and over, spins around and sits, dangling her legs.

"That," says Tully from across the gym, "is called a cat-hang. That is one way you can enter Room 3.14. But for today, you may walk."

I wonder if this is some crazy circus performer class. Kids sit atop a balance beam like birds on a wire, others are on the blue floor. Trace is on the opposite side of the gym from Bree, on top of a pyramid with a flat top, like a huge triangle-shaped cake with the tip sliced off.

"Grab a spot, anywhere you like, Jeremy," Tully says.

I step onto a padded blue surface that is raised up off the floor. Tully explains that the blue platform is spring-loaded. The whole floor rests on springs that absorb shock. This is definitely circus class.

"Welcome to Room 3.14. This is your most important class of the day. This is Parkour." Tully writes PARKOUR on a whiteboard.

"For you literal types, the French word Parkour literally means, the way through. Parkour is the sport of moving from one point to another with speed and efficiency, using the natural abilities of the human body."

While Tully is talking, Bree and Trace are in motion. Or, more accurately, in flight. It looks like their feet don't touch the ground before they're in the air again, moving from building-to-bar-to-wall like jumping frogs.

"Parkour movements, such as those you see on the course that Bree and Trace are demonstrating, help stimulate your neural networks. Parkour is where you will make connections, overcome obstacles, and see the way through difficult tasks. You'll mark your study of Parkour as a beginning," Tully says.

Beginning of what? I wonder.

"Give us another run through, please," Tully calls to Bree and Trace.

Trace goes first, running across the platform floor toward a cushion that is four feet high and looks like a huge blue vinyl mattress. At the edge of the cushion is a small trampoline tilted at a slight angle. On the wall behind the cushion are horizontal bars, like a wide ladder. Trace runs across the floor, leaps and touches the edge of the trampoline, flips forward heels over head onto the mattress where he lands on his feet. He jumps onto the ladder, climbing to the very top rung. He spins in the air; does another flip forward, and lands on his feet.

A girl sitting next to me mumbles under her breath, "I am not doing that."

I recognize her from the MPR as the girl that folded her paper into a triangle football and launched it across the table.

"Hot lava!" shouts Tully. "The floor is hot lava. Your goal is to stay off the floor and move across it without burning your toes. Let's go, first up."

The girl next to me crosses her arms defiantly. A boy pushes himself off the beam and walks to the mark on the floor where Bree and Trace launched.

"Hot Lava," Tully repeats. "Go!" The boy takes off but doesn't leave enough room to get a solid landing on the trampoline, so he stops just short of it, jumps, does a clumsy roll onto the mat, then struggles to get up again. He takes two steps across the mattress, grasps the bars and climbs up three rungs. He hesitates before letting go and, when he falls, his arms splay out to the sides.

Tully yells, "Next up!" and motions to the kid on the other end of the beam.

"Hot lava! Feet off the ground," Tully reminds us. I watch every kid misjudge the distance to the trampoline, so they don't get any propulsion from it. Doesn't anyone here know how energy works? When the girl next to me takes her turn, she doesn't run. She walks. She walks all the way to the trampoline, steps on it, does a lazy somersault, stands up, touches the ladder with one finger and then steps off the mattress.

Tully signals me to go. I land on the trampoline with both feet, but I'm disappointed in how little bounce it gives me. I try the front flip the way Trace did it only I land flat on my back. I pop up to grab the ladder. I climb all the way to the top. Higher than anyone else did.

I let go and fall. I am confident for this part because falling is my superpower.

Next, Tully instructs us to climb up the side of a pyramid, jump feet first into the pit of foam, then climb out, shimmy up another ladder and sit on the wall, where Bree first sat dangling her legs. Bree, who is now skipping across the bars with light feet and crossing the room, shows off while Trace and Tully shout encouragement to the next kid in line.

All of us make it to the wall. From up here, the gym looks like a Minecraft set, with trenches and walls and bars and angular obstacles. We are the little miner dwarfs doing our jobs, scurrying through another day in search of food and elements to build our cabins.

"Well done!" Tully exclaims. "You have each just demonstrated many of the principles of physics. Linear motion and rotational motion. From the moment of inertia to the conservation of energy."

Beside me, the girl draws in her breath and whispers, "Oh! I get it! This is like science class."

When Tully calls for a volunteer, she is the first one to leap down from the wall.

CHAPTER 12

THE GOD OF ROOFTOPS

When I was four, I fell off the roof. Specifically, I fell through the roof, by way of a skylight.

Dad left a ladder leaning against the side of the house, and I climbed up, surprised at how easy it was. I walked over the staggered black roof shingles and peered into my own bedroom window. Then I went to the ladder and looked down. Getting down was going to be scarier than going up. I wandered around on the rooftop until it was dark. It was the first time I saw my world in one big view. I could see my street all the way down to the park at the end. I was the God of Rooftops, and this was my domain to rule. I was all powerful. I could see everything coming before it could sneak up on me. Mom and Dad were walking around outside calling my name. I don't know why I did it, but I did not answer them. I sat on the roof, watching the cars roll down the street as the sky darkened and the stars appeared until my Dad's head appeared at the top of the ladder.

"Hey there, Jeremy. Whatcha doing up here?"

I didn't answer.

"Let's get down now. Can you come over to the ladder?" I could get to the ladder, yes, but I didn't want to. The stars dotted the night sky. It was the best part of the day, and I had a new place to watch it all unfold. My kingdom.

Dad got onto the roof and walked toward me with careful steps. I scooted away, crab walking away from him. As he came closer to me and made a grab for my leg, I crab-walked right onto the skylight. That's when I heard a shattering crack, like a dropped glass jar of jelly on the tile floor. The skylight broke apart and collapsed underneath me.

The scary part wasn't falling. It wasn't even hitting the bottom. It was the horrified look on Mom's face when I hit the kitchen floor with a thud. I let out a wail as she rushed to brush glass away from me. Dad ran in a few seconds later.

I suffered a few bruises and scratches, but that was nothing. Mom and Dad fought for days, then stopped talking to each other, because they couldn't agree whose fault it was that I fell through the skylight.

I learned two things.

One: Even though Dad made me practice going up and down the ladder, my bedroom window was the easiest way to get on and off the roof.

Two: Falling isn't all that scary, but the landing? That takes practice.

When we leave Room 3.14, I'm sweaty and a little shaky, and it is time for lunch. I unzip my new lunch box expecting to see the familiar prepackaged meal with ham and crackers and a chocolate peanut butter cup. Nope. My mom has packed deli ham in a baggie, whole almonds and sliced apples which are turning brown. No crackers. I don't eat ham without crackers. Plus, this isn't the ham I like. It's darker in color, and instead of being cut into a perfect circle to fit on a round cracker, it's crumpled thinly sliced meat. I quickly hide the napkin where Mom has written Good Luck! I love you! before anyone sees it. I zip up my lunch box and don't eat anything. My stomach is full, anyway.

"You're not going to eat?" Trace asks. I shake my head. He hands me something from his lunch box. It's a protein bar.

"Try this. It's got non-dairy chocolate chips."

I take a bite, and it's better than I expect, so I eat a couple more bites. But my stomach is a balled-up fist. No room for food.

"Meds?" He asks.

I nod. How did he know?

"Which one?"

"The blue one."

"Ah, yes. The first couple of weeks are the worst. It gets better, though. You should try to eat something."

It hasn't occurred to me that the little blue pill I tried to wipe off my tongue could be the cause.

We are walking down the hall when someone tugs on my shirt. I turn around to see a boy looking at my shoes. It's the little boy that sat with Bree. He has long blond hair to his shoulders, and some of it falls over his face. For a second, I think I am looking at a smaller version of me.

"You're it," he says, extending his index finger and touching me lightly on the arm. Then he runs.

Trace, Ben and David laugh. "That's Jeremy," says Ben. "We're going to have to call you something else, now."

"Or, we have to call that Jeremy something else," says David, pointing to the little boy as he disappears around the corner.

"Jeremy the Younger!" Trace exclaims. "He likes you. He never touches anything he doesn't like."

"He's Bree's baby brother," David chimes in. "No one ever messes with him."

We arrive at a classroom I recognize from the tour and Trace says, "This is your room for the fifth period. It's first-timers class. You only go for the first week, then you'll be with Ruthenium element again."

In first-timers class, there are kids of all ages. They roam around the room playing with stuff in Distraction Station. Some have metal puzzles. Others play on a piano. A boy is upside down on the sofa with a Rubik's Cube. Two girls sit crisscross-applesauce on the floor playing chess. One kid draws diagrams of molecules on a dry erase board.

Trace must have made a mistake. I've wandered into daycare. I am backing out of the room when a voice calls out.

"Welcome, Jeremy! Please come in and get comfortable."

I spot the teacher, who is on his knees with a boy sorting bins full of interlocking circuits.

"Come on in! We'll get started with class in five minutes. Meanwhile, it's free thinking time." Then he calls to the boy who is upside down on the sofa. "Let's hear it for vestibular and proprioceptive sensory input, aye, Stanley?" The boy on the sofa twists away at the cube and gives a slight nod.

I liked this room last week when it wasn't full of children. I don't know anyone. There are desks and chairs, but no one is sitting in them. It's like free time, but there is so much to look at I don't know what to do. Therefore, I do what works in this situation. I back up to the wall and slide down to the floor. I pull my knees up to my chest and wrap my arms around my knees. It's the only way I know how to be still.

It only takes a few minutes for the first kid to wander my way. It's the upside-down kid named Stanley. He pokes my knee. I notice his red hair.

"What are you supposed to be?" He asks.

I spring to life and wave my arms like a monster, roaring at him. Stanley jumps back, startled. At first, I think he is going to cry. Then he nods.

"I get it. You're a monster. That's not very original." He holds out the Rubik's Cube. "I got one side done. Green. Where's yours?"

I take mine out of my pack and show him.

"You don't have any sides yet." He twists it slowly to demonstrate. "You do it like this."

He moves the green side out of place, but as he does, the white side comes together.

"You have to mess it up before you can fix it right again," he explains. "Plus, it helps to know the algorithms. I'm still learning them."

The teacher calls for attention and sorts everyone into groups, mixing in younger kids with older kids, then pointing us to tables with our names taped to them. I am at a table with Stanley, a little girl name Gemma and an empty chair named Hazel.

The door opens, and a girl walks in. It's the girl from Room 3.14. The one who whispered, I get it! I catch a glimpse of Dr. Nugent closing the door behind her.

The teacher waves her in and motions to my table.

"Come on in, Hazel. Right here next to Jeremy."

Hazel sits down. She looks like she's been crying. She turns to me with excitement in her voice.

"I threw up in the girls' bathroom. This place is amazing, don't you think?"

CHAPTER 13

FIRST TIMER'S CLASS

Welcome to First Timer's Class, a bald man named Mr. Turnbull writes.

"Who likes rules?" He asks loudly. Stanley raises his hand.

"Stanley likes rules. Why do you like rules, Stanley?"

"I don't like rules," Stanley says. "I like the idea of rules, but most rules are wrong in one way or another."

Stanley sounds like a grown-up with a tiny voice. His small hands twist the cube as he speaks and his thin face seems incapable of smiling without being given specific directions.

Mr. Turnbull nods thoughtfully. "Other thoughts about rules? Yes, Gemma."

The miniature girl next to me says, "Rules have exceptions. So, they aren't really rules if there are exceptions."

"Interesting," Mr. Turnbull responds. "What if we change the word 'rules' to be something we all agree with? What would that be?"

Stanley says, "It would be impossible."

"Let's try it, anyway. Try the word *truth* in place of the word *rules*." He draws a stick figure, then points the marker at Hazel.

"Hazel, what do you see?"

"A zombie?" she says after studying the drawing.

Stanley chimes in, "Circle and lines."

Gemma raises her hand. "His head is too big for his body."

Suddenly everyone in the class wants to say something about the drawing. Hands go up, and excited talking erupts. I cover my ears and lower my throbbing head.

"Truth #1!" Mr. Turnbull says loudly. "There are no wrong answers."

That brings silence.

"Hazel saw a person of undead origin. Not a boy, not a girl, but a person. Stanley saw shapes. A circle and some lines. Gemma saw proportions. A head that doesn't seem right for the body supporting it. These are all correct answers to the question, *what do you see?* But, if I ask the question differently, such as *what is this?* All of these answers are wrong."

"There are no wrong answers," Mr. Turnbull emphasizes. "There are only wrong questions."

Next to me, Hazel claps her hands and gives a little squeal. Hands shoot up in the air.

"Not in math! Not in history!" Say numerous voices. Stanley looks up. He nods his head and says, "Science."

"Mathematics, science, history, all those things you are talking about, those are covered in Truth Number Four. Now for Truth Number Two." He writes *Labels limit people.*

Mr. Turnbull points the marker at me. "Jeremy, give us an example of a label."

My head is still pounding and with my palms pressed on my temples. I hate labels in my clothing because they bother me so much that I can't think. I answer him, "Things that bother me."

"Indeed. Labels bother me, too. Other examples of labels?"

Hands shoot up, and kids shout answers. They're on soup cans. They're in shirts, and my mom cuts them out. They list the ingredients. They are required by the FDA. That one was Stanley.

Mr. Turnbull asks a question. "Labels tell you what's inside, right? So, if you had to put a label on yourself, what would it say?" No one responds. Stanley stops twisting his cube and stares at the table.

"Anyone?" Mr. Turnbull asks. "Is there a label that tells us what is inside you?" I stare at my hands and don't answer. It's like trying to name every star in the sky.

I can hear a few mumbled answers that sound like illnesses and others that sound like insults. Like Hazel, who whispers, "Stubborn."

"I don't like labels," Stanley pipes, "because they don't tell you everything."

Mr. Turnbull gazes at a silent classroom.

"I don't like them either, Stanley. That's how we feel about labels at Equator School. Many of you may be used to describing yourselves with labels that a teacher, another student, or an adult have used to describe you. Sometimes those labels are necessary, like when you are talking to your doctor. Other times, labels make you feel like there is something wrong with you."

Heads bob around the room.

Mr. Turnbull says, "Truth Number Two is *Labels Limit People.*" No one disagrees.

Truth Number Three is *Kindness Heals,* which cheers everyone up immediately.

"Name some ways you can show kindness," Turnbull says. The class bubbles with answers that are not wrong. Share your lunch. Tell someone they look nice. Don't hit. Draw a picture of a puppy. Take turns. Be quiet. Be good. Clap. Flush.

"And if you can't think of something kind to do, *ask,*" Mr. Turnbull says. "Asking someone, how can I help you? That's also a kindness."

Truth Number Four is *Answers Evolve.*

"This is the basis of science and many other things we seek to discover," Mr. Turnbull says. "Think about the labels you have heard about yourself. Are they true? How would you prove or disprove them?"

Stanley speaks. "Look in my brain."

Gemma asks excitedly, "Do we get to look at brains?"

"Yes!" Mr. Turnbull booms. This brings a whole lot of talking all at once. "And lots of other things too. Is there only one way to reach checkmate? Is there only one theory about the origins of life? Is there more than one way to make a fusion reactor? Only one way in and out of this classroom? All truths can be reached even if by different paths."

Several kids clap their hands.

"The last Truth, Number Five, is undefined. It's for you to decide. It's the thing that belongs inside here." He erases the stick person and draws a big circle on the board.

"Your own personal truth. It's the most important thing about you. It's your purpose. It's the reason you are here. We are all explorers, and this is our trailhead."

Mr. Turnbull smiles broadly, throws out his arms like he wants to hug the room and proclaims, "Welcome to the journey to you!"

CHAPTER 14

SOFT LANDINGS

At the end of the day, I am hungry, tired, my head buzzes, and my ears are ringing. I wait outside at parent pickup. Trace races by and stops just long enough to offer me a fist bump, which I miss, and then he leaps into a minivan. I see Hazel get in a car and hug her mom like she hasn't seen her for a year. When my mom pulls up, I climb in the backseat and lay down on it like a pillow.

"Hey there! How was your first day? Would you like to go for ice cream?"

"No."

I don't tell her that I feel sick because then she'll ask me zillions of questions. I barely hear her respond, "No, *thank you.*"

I fall asleep on my backpack, and I don't hear anything else until Mom wakes me up at the apartment. When we get inside, I go to my room and climb up into my bunk. I scrunch up my pillow into a lump the way I like it and fall asleep.

It's dark when I wake up. Mom is asleep. I am still wearing my shoes. I go to the kitchen for something to eat and find a note Mom left on the table.

Look in the fridge. XO Mom.

In the fridge is a plate with a dish of yogurt, sliced strawberries and some scrunched up slices of ham. I'd rather it was a sandwich, but there is no real bread anywhere, just a gluten-free brick. I eat the yogurt and strawberries and nibble on the ham.

It's not enough to make me sleepy. I'm bored and awake, two of the worst things to be at the same time. It's a good time to go up on the roof and count some stars.

Counting stars is a game. Like all games, it has rules. I get to make up the rules because it's my game and I'm the only one playing. I get to decide if the weakly lit stars count as a full star. I get to decide if they are stars, satellites, aircraft or space junk hurtling toward the planet. If I get bored from counting (and I do, sometimes), I pretend to draw lines from star to star. Or I sort the stars by color, size, and shape. Sometimes I close my eyes and listen for the stars to sing like science thinks they can.

The stars sing quiet songs, like dust in the air that floats by the kitchen window when the bright light pours in. The sound of the stars is a shushing that fills my ears. Ideas appear in my head like gifts. Big ideas. Small, dim ideas. Some are bright and hot. And the colorful ones? They are practically combustible. That's the night sky. It's more than sparkling dots. It's scattered ideas that need sorting. Some good ideas.

Some bad ideas. And some that you really shouldn't try before asking your mom.

On my second day at Equator School, we are herded into the MPR when we arrive for *morning kickstart*. The purple stars are at the door handing out plastic bags with stuff in them. The kid who hands me a bag reminds me to put my name tag on, but I've lost it. I take the bag and sit in the back of the room, as close to the door as I can get. I always feel better when I know the way out. I look around the room and see Jeremy the Younger sitting next to Bree and digging in his own bag.

Tully's voice carries across the room as I look in the bag and see ... sticky notes?

"Good morning! Welcome to morning kickstart, day two. You may now commence your survival kit swap for the next ten minutes."

Bags are dumped on the tables, and the room swirls with movement. My bag has a hacky sack and a small wooden puzzle, a felt square with two marbles sewn inside, a package of sunflower seeds, and a package of breath mints. I'm still examining my loot when a kid approaches me.

"Do you want your sunflower seeds?" He's already holding five tube-shaped packages. I hand mine over. He offers me my choice of yellow sticky notes, mechanical pencil lead or a pack of gum. I take the gum, because, when do you ever get to have gum in school?

When I sit down in Chemistry, I keep my left hand under the desk as I feel the smooth and bumpy surface of a small rubber ball. Doing anything with my right hand is impossible. While I struggle to draw a picture of a hydrogen atom, Mrs. Yaw, comes to my desk and points to my left hand. I open my palm, let out a sigh and hand her the ball.

She smiles and closes my fist with her fingers.

"It's okay. You don't have to hide it. For those of you who are new to fidgets, you can relax. It's okay to use them however you feel comfortable."

Other hands that are under the desk slowly come out clutching their fidgets. Bree coughs out a laugh from across the room. *Loser* is what I hear.

Mrs. Yaw looks at her patiently.

"Bree, that's one."

Bree has no fidget in her hand. She doesn't do anything like jiggle her leg or tap her pen or chew on her hair the way everyone else does. She is perfectly still. She focuses an unwavering stare at Mrs. Yaw, who returns only a kind smile.

In Room 3.14, Trace and Bree are in the center of the springy floor. I stand next to Hazel who is excitedly bouncing up and down on her toes. Tully is talking. He does a lot of talking.

"Today you will learn the most basic and important two moves in Parkour. Parkour can be dangerous. You will miss your marks, and you'll get bruises. You'll crash a lot. Therefore, the first thing we are practicing is how to land."

Both Trace and Bree, cued by Tully, leap into the air, knees bent to their chests, like frogs, and come down into a squat. Tully points out how they land on the balls of their feet. Then he makes us all show him that we know what the balls of our feet are.

One at a time, we frog-leap into the air and land with our arms thrust forward, letting our legs bend to absorb the shock. We do it five times, leaping from one side of the room to the other. I am surprised how hard it is to launch your entire body off the ground without anything to make it go.

Trace demonstrates the next thing that Tully says will come in handy to not break an arm. It's called a safety roll. You do it when you are coming down from somewhere high to make a soft landing. As you come down, your knees are bent, and arms are rounded like you are picking up a trashcan. You roll from your shoulder to your opposite hip, pop up onto your feet, and whammo, you're not hurt. We practice that one five times across the room, each way. I watch Trace and Bree safety roll and barely skim the surface of the mat before they pop up onto their feet. The other kids are afraid of coming down on their heads and twist their bodies so that they flop on their butts and can't pop up.

Hazel is flat on her back on the floor, one arm flung over her eyes. I nudge her with my foot.

"Are you going to throw up again?"

She peers up at me. "Maybe, but I don't care."

Trace checks on her. "She's good," he says. "I recommend not eating too much before this class. That's why lunch is next and not before."

When we leave room 3.14 for lunch, I am not nauseated. Trace races past me and turns around, running backward while he talks.

"Hey, you're good at this," he says, then turns and runs off.

I let the words sit in the air before I suck them in with one breath.

I am good at this.

Not falling.

Landing.

CHAPTER 15

PIECE OF CAKE

"What is a goal?" Mr. Turnbull asks in first-timers' class.

Hazel's hand shoots up. "When you get a point, like in soccer."

"Perfect!" He turns to the board and draws a goal post. "I love soccer! Let's talk about soccer. Before you ever get that ball kicked through the posts, what do you have to do?"

Gemma raises her hand. "You have to steal it from someone else."

Mr. Turnbull writes it on the board. "Good! What else? Call them out, everyone."

Everyone shouts out answers. Buy a ball. Kick the ball down the field. Pass it to a teammate. Snag it when it comes your way. Sneak it past the goalie. Mr. Turnbull draws pictures and writes words on the board as fast as he can.

"Now, what happens before you ever step on the field?"

Gemma speaks up again. "You put on the tall socks."

"And even before that, what happens?"

Hazel says, "You practice."

Mr. Turnbull looked like he could burst with happiness. "And before that? Jeremy, any thoughts?"

Once when Dad and I were on our way to Dave's Burger

Joint for guy time, we passed a soccer field full of kids in green and yellow uniforms. Parents sat under pop-up shades with coolers and lawn chairs. It looked like a party. I wanted so much to be one of those kids. I asked Dad if I could play soccer, too.

He didn't answer right away. He was having a cigarette. It always took him a long time to answer when he was smoking.

"You have a soccer ball in the garage."

I knew I had one, but other than kicking it around the backyard by myself I never did anything with it. Kicking a ball around by yourself is boring. I kicked it into Mom's lemon tree, and she yelled at me, so I stopped. The ball eventually went flat in the garage.

Mr. Turnbull says my name again. "Jeremy? Any answer will do."

"I don't play soccer."

Hazel elbows me and whispers, "Join a team."

"Join a team?" I say.

Mr. Turnbull draws a big circle around all the pictures and words written about soccer.

"If you want to score a goal, it takes a team," he says. "All these things inside the circle happen when you work together. Let's try it. I have a game."

Me, Hazel, Gemma, and Stanley are a team. Every team gets

one whiteboard, and Mr. Turnbull says we can write or draw our answers.

"Your task, as a team, is to figure out how to reach your goal." He walks around to each group with slips of paper in his hand, fanned out like playing cards. Each team chooses one. Gemma pulls a strip of paper from his hands and reads it excitedly.

"Bake a cake! I know how to do that!" Gemma draws a picture of a cake. "I make cakes at home with my mom!"

Stanley, who is immersed in his Rubik's cube, comments, "I don't like chocolate."

"I don't like chocolate, either," I say. It's true. I don't.

Hazel asks, thoughtfully, "Who is the cake for?"

Gemma says quickly, "The homeless man that's out there at the bus stop every morning."

Suddenly, Stanley is intensely interested in the conversation. "Does he like chocolate? Because if he likes chocolate, then I'm okay with that."

"But what's his name?" Gemma asks with concern. "We need to know his name."

Mr. Turnbull comes by to see how we are doing. He listens to us talk before he chimes in.

"His name is Frank. And yes, he likes chocolate. What do you need to do first if you want to bake Frank a chocolate cake?"

We list all the things that we must do. Buy cake mix. Get a bowl and a spoon. Find the kitchen. Borrow a cake pan from Gemma's mom. After we have a long list of things to do, Mr. Turnbull tells us to put them in order.

When class ends, we have made a list of everything from the brand of cake mix that Gemma likes best to the colors of the sprinkles on the frosting after it is baked. Hazel will get all the ingredients. Gemma wants to mix it. Stanley wants to put it in the oven, set the timer and take it out to cool. We all want to help frost and decorate it. I'm elected to deliver the cake to Frank.

It's a bummer that we aren't really going to bake a chocolate cake for homeless Frank. It's just an exercise. When we leave the room, Stanley stops me at the door and holds up his cube. He's got a third side, yellow, completed.

"Hey, that's great, Stanley."

"Piece of cake," he replies, and I'm not sure he knows he just made a wicked pun.

Chapter 16

Things Not Spoken

That afternoon at parent pickup, Bree, and Jeremy the Younger stand close to me. He looks so small. He's drawing in a sketchbook and standing in Bree's shadow. I've noticed he doesn't like to stand in direct sunlight like he's a Zombie that's going to incinerate.

I reach around Bree and tap him on the shoulder.

"You're it."

He giggles without looking up from his sketchbook. Bree smacks my hand away.

"Don't touch him. He doesn't like it," she says sharply.

"He laughed."

She glares at me. "*I* don't like it."

Bree makes me nervous. I put my hand into my pocket to find the marbles and walk away.

Trace, Ben, and David approach laughing and talking.

"Hey," Trace says. He nods at Bree, who glares at him and grabs her little brother by the backpack, the shoves him in the direction of her dad's car.

David says, "Man, I hate her."

Ben nudges him. "Don't say hate."

"Okay. I am strongly the opposite of liking her," David retorts and Ben nods in approval.

Trace is looking at me. I have both hands in my pockets now.

"What's wrong?"

It's all familiar. The first week of school I make a new enemy, just by being me.

"Nothing."

Trace looks like he doesn't believe me.

"Okay. See ya." He hops into his mom's minivan.

Just then my mom pulls up. When I get in the car, she asks, "Are those new friends?"

I lay down on my backpack and close my eyes.

"I don't know."

That night, when I wake up hungry and eat the plate of food that Mom left for me in the fridge, I can't get back to sleep. The sky is overcast, and the stars are blocked. My head is cloudy, too. I sit on the roof but it's not the same, so I climb back down and go to the playground. My thoughts bounce like popping corn. *School is weird. Trace might be a friend. Bree might be insane. I think someone needs to look out for Jeremy the Younger. I think someone needs to look out for...*

I am about to insert to *my mom*. Instead, the words that jump in are *my dad*. I try not to think about my dad, but he slips in there anyway. He's the root beer bottle cap in my pocket. A thing I fidget with that makes me think he's coming back. It also makes me think I am weird and stupid.

The play structure is on a rubber mat made from shredded tires. The surface gets too hot in the daytime but, at night, it's perfect. Three platforms lead to a pirate's lair with a ship wheel and a pretend telescope. It's really for babies. But whatever. No one else is around. I stand on the first level platform and practice safety rolls. Knees up. Shoulder down. Roll from shoulder to hip and pop up again.

I practice an underbar through the window of the pirate ship. We learned underbar in 3.14 today. Get a running start. Feet go first, grab the bar (or the window top) but not too soon, or you lose the momentum. Body is almost horizontal when you slide through the gap. Over and over I go until the clouds in my head are gone, and I can see the stars in my brain. Even though I don't know where they are leading me, it feels like a map that only makes sense when I'm *not* trying to make sense of it.

I lay flat on my back on the highest platform and listen to my heart pounding. I count one hundred heartbeats.

When I get back home the light is on in the kitchen. Mom is sitting at the table drinking tea. It's late. I'm in trouble.

But she doesn't say anything, she holds her mug close to her chin, inhaling the steam and smiles at me. I sit down on a kitchen chair next to her. When she reaches over to move the hair away from my eyes, I don't jerk away like I usually do. I think she is about to tell me something. We've had a lot of these talks.

"You need to try harder."

"What's going on with you?"

"I heard from your homeroom teacher today."

Whatever it is, I don't want to hear it. I just spent all that time outside clearing the clutter out of my head. Unless it's the words, "Your dad is coming home," I am not interested.

But she says nothing. She sips her tea. I stare at the table. I'm too sleepy to figure out what this silence means. My heart pumps slower. I count heartbeats until I can't keep track. I put my head in my arms on the table, face down, and close my eyes. Still, she doesn't say anything. When she gets up to go to bed, she pauses and kisses me on the head.

It's probably the best conversation we've ever had.

CHAPTER 17

BOSSY SNOBSTER

What was Tully thinking?

Tully leaves Bree and Trace in charge in Room 3.14. We are split into groups, and I'm in Bree's group. I can tell she absolutely loves the fact she is in charge by the way she holds her head above everyone else's, hands on her hips, feet shoulder-width apart, daring any one of us to move without her permission. Hazel is also in Bree's group. Bree commands us like an Army platoon, demanding we stand in a straight line for inspection, while she walks slowly down the line finding something to correct about everyone.

For Hazel, it's her new shoes. She showed them to me this morning. They are canvas shoes painted to look like a starry galaxy with silver shoelaces. She calls them her galaxy shoes.

"Those shoes are wrong for so many reasons. Take them off. You're better off barefoot," Bree orders. "Plus, they're ugly."

"*You're* ugly," Hazel responds. "I'll wear whatever I want."

Bree doesn't even flinch. "Look, Hazelnut, you'll take off those kindergartner bling shoes that will guarantee you a broken shinbone, or you can sit out the class."

Bree walks down the line and inspects everyone's shoes.

"Laces. Hard plastic arch. Soles are too thick. No arch. Light ups? Seriously, how old are you?" She comes back to Hazel who has not removed her shoes.

"Yours are everything a Parkour shoe is not. The soles are too thick, so your feet can't find their position. There are no arches to stop you sliding forward over an edge. Shall I continue?"

Hazel takes in a deep, angry breath through flared nostrils and says, "You don't have to be a bossy snobster about it." I can't help it. I snort with laughter. I let my wall of hair hide my face when Bree slides over and looks down her pointy nose at me.

"Empty your pockets, freak show."

I shake my head. My hair sways from side to side. She can't see my eyes. She leans in close to my ear and whispers, "Do it, or I'll crush you like the scared little bug you are."

My heart pounding, I whisper back to her.

"Bossy snobster."

Hazel cracks up next to me and Bree, furious, shoves me back with both arms.

"Hey, hey, that's not cool." Trace runs over and jumps between Bree and me. "Jeremy, you and Hazel can be in my group. Bree, you take Joey and Elisa."

Joey and Elisa look at each other like they would rather do

cartwheels on a bed of nails, then slowly trudge over to Bree's group.

"Thanks, guys, I'll make it up to you, I promise," Trace says to them.

"Where is Tully? Why would he leave *her* in charge?" Hazel fumes.

Trace says calmly, "It's all good now, let's just get started with conditioning, okay?"

I don't know how Trace does it. He never misses an opportunity to be the good guy. On the one hand, I really want to be his friend. On the other hand, I suspect he just feels sorry for me.

"Dude, your hair is cool, but it's going to get you hurt. You need to be able to see what's coming. I suggest, uh, a ponytail maybe? If you don't want to cut it, that is."

Hazel interjects, "I have a ponytail holder in my backpack."

"No, thanks," I say quietly. I feel even less like showing my face now. Something flies at my head. Bree has launched a ball cap at me. She sticks out her tongue.

"Nice. Mature," Trace mumbles. "Uh, there you go. Try that," he says. "Wear it backward, so it doesn't mess up your line of sight, or sideways, which is, you know, gangster."

I can't tell if he is joking or serious. I put the hat on backward.

"Okay, now that's settled, like my colleague said, please empty your pockets so that stuff doesn't fall out and create a hazard for everyone else."

I'm relieved when we go outside away from Bree. Trace instructs us to jump from one planter wall to another. The walls are only about two feet tall, and there are two of them, about six feet apart, lining the front walk to the school. After that, we practice going up and down stairs three at a time.

It's about 100°F outside. We tire out fast and break for water as soon as we get through the first rotation. After cooling off, we go again. Hazel, still wearing the wrong shoes, slips while jumping from the planter wall. She crashes into the wall on the other side. Her shin is scraped and bloody, but she gets up and walks to a shady spot. Trace hands her a cold bottle of water, and she rinses her shin.

"Good job, everyone. Let's move it back inside and hook up with Bree's group for some vault practice."

Hazel limps in behind the group, and I fall back to walk with her.

"You okay?"

"I'm fine," she says crossly. "I wasn't paying attention."

"You couldn't have done it barefoot anyway. You'd burn your feet."

"I'm an idiot. I hate that bossy snobster was right. So, are you going to cut your hair?"

"Maybe. I don't know. A ball cap is okay, I guess."

Trace comes up behind us and claps a hand on Hazel's shoulder.

"How's your leg?" He hands Hazel a fistful of bandages.

"It's fine. Who leaves *her* in charge? I mean is this a school? Is it a lunatic asylum?"

I've noticed that Hazel manages to say what I can't. I don't even realize she is saying what I'm thinking until I hear the words. I can't pull sentences out of my head like she can. Trace smiles patiently. I wonder if he is searching his head for the words, too.

"It's definitely different here. Give it time."

I can see why Tully trusts Trace with our group. But, I also agree with Hazel. What kind of place lets a bossy snobster be in charge?

At lunch, Jeremy the Younger slips next to me as I line up to buy something to eat because I forgot my lunch box. There are bananas, apples, cheese, veggies and gluten-free stuff that you need a gallon of water to wash down. Do humans actually eat kale chips? I'd kill for a bag of pork rinds.

I've learned that wherever Jeremy the Younger is, Bree isn't far away. It's like he's on an invisible leash, the kind that you can reel back in when the critter gets too far away from you.

Today, he hands me a note.

"You're it," he whispers, then dodges back into line next to his sister. Inside the note is a picture of a face. Kind of a creepy face, too. The note says: *Meet me in Room 3.14 after school. Important.*

It doesn't have Bree's name on it, but I know it's her. Not just because it was delivered by her brother. Because the face in the picture has strange, empty circles where eyes should be.

CHAPTER 18

THE BIG PICTURE

It's the last first-timers' class. Stanley is upside down on the sofa again, twisting away at his Rubik's Cube. He's got three sides solved. Turnbull writes one word on the board, then he draws a circle around it and says it out loud.

"Why."

I groan and put my head down on the desk. Hazel elbows me.

"You can do this. Pretend it's a lazy vault. You are awesome at those."

A lazy vault is when you run alongside a wall, lean your body back like you are going to fall, then throw the leg closest to the wall over, followed by the other leg. It all happens in about half a second if you do it correctly. Your wall-side hand and wall-side leg both get you over and the second leg just follows. Then you're off and running. I fail to see how why is anything like a lazy vault.

"The hard part is making the first move to go over the wall, right? Pretend that what's on the other side of the wall is something you want more than anything. What do you want so much you'd vault over a wall for it?"

I wish it were that easy. I wish that everything was as easy as vaulting over a wall. I wonder if Hazel can see through my wall of hair and into my brain, where everything I love burns to ash. What do I want? That's not even answerable.

"Draw a picture inside a circle," she suggests. "You don't have to say it out loud."

My face gets hot like the fire in my head is about to burst out of my eyeballs.

"Okay, I get it," I say crossly and Hazel looks away with a hurt look on her face. But I don't get it.

Turnbull is watching. He moves in front of my desk and says, "What part is holding you back, Jeremy?"

I don't even look up. Turnbull doesn't give up and walks away like teachers usually do when I can't answer their questions. He asks a different question.

"Think of something that makes you feel good. What does that look like to you?"

I think about that for a bit. Then I have an answer, sort of. It's the only answer I can come up with, and I am afraid it is stupid, so I don't say it immediately. Turnbull waits patiently even though another girl is waving her hand from across the room.

"Do you remember Truth Number One?" he prompts. I don't. I shake my head a tiny bit.

Hazel whispers to me, "There are no wrong answers, only wrong questions."

I am still nervous that my answer is stupid and a wrong answer, but now I'm more nervous because both Turnbull, Hazel and the girl waving her hand are all waiting for me.

"The sky, I guess. The stars," I mumble.

Turnbull grins. "Aha. A big picture thinker. It's no wonder you cannot fit your why into that tiny circle. Where others see the sun, the moon, a cloud, a star, you, Jeremy, see a universe."

Jeremy the Younger is chasing a playground ball around the maze of walls and bars in Room 3.14. Bree appears with a cat-like, silent landing. She's dropped down from a bar overhead. Jeremy the Younger runs over and points up to the top of the bar.

"Not today," she says. "I'm busy."

He makes a pouty face and runs back to his ball.

"He doesn't talk much," I say.

"You just don't speak his language," she retorts. "You figured it out yet?"

Her voice changes from scorn to sweet. But I don't trust that. I don't look at her because I'm watching Jeremy the Younger kick his ball against a wall and get hit in the gut on its return. He whimpers.

"Oh, I get it. You don't make transitions well. I know the type." She gestures to her little brother. "Get over it because I have something important to tell you,"

I walk past her to Jeremy the Younger, who is now sitting crisscross on the floor with his ball, his head sunk into his palms.

I sit down across from him, but not too close. I crawl across the floor and reach my hand out and tap him on the knee.

"You're it," I say.

"Hey, I am talking to you," Bree protests.

Jeremy the Younger is talking to me now. He looks up and smiles, even though he isn't looking directly at me, I know that something in his brain can see that I'm not going to be mean to him. He rolls me the ball. I roll it back to him. He does it again. I roll it back.

"He's not a baby," Bree says, stepping in between us and picking up the ball. He growls in protest. She throws the ball over his head and points at it.

"Go fetch, we have business to discuss."

"He's not a puppy." I watch Jeremy the Younger lope off into a corner of the maze walls, going after the ball. I cross my arms and glare at her. "What do you want?"

"In the next week, things are going to change. If you want to be on the winning side of the game, you would be wise to ditch that crowd you've glommed onto and stick with me."

"Game?"

"Team captain selection. It's going to be me or Trace because we are the most experienced. Plus, we're the only students here who aren't terrified to speak out loud."

When I don't say anything, she says impatiently, "This isn't like a regular school. If you want to move up, you must show that you can be a part of a team. Do I really need to explain this to you?"

When I don't answer, she says, "Nominate me for team captain, and I'll make sure you pass seventh grade."

I'm quiet, but she keeps talking, pacing back and forth in front of me.

"I'm trying to help you out. The fourth hour is experimental. The fourth hour is where they figure out what you can do. I don't mean can you do math or speak nine languages. More like, what are you good at? For Trace and me, it's Parkour. David and Ben are in theater. My baby brother is in art. There's also rock band, engineering, and math team."

"No thanks. I'm good," I say.

"Look, here's the deal. Nominate me for me for the class captain, not only will I make sure you pass all your classes, I'll make sure no one finds out what you did."

That's it. I turn away from her, pick up my backpack and walk towards the door.

"Everyone here failed at regular school. We're all a bunch of misfits, you know. Everyone here has something to hide."

How could she know what I did? I've seen her talking privately with Dr. Nugent. Would Dr. Nugent tell her why I'm here?

Bree changes her tone and pleads. "I want to help you be successful here. You won't pass without my help. I've got connections."

Great. Another way to fail.

"I don't understand what you want from me." I am watching Jeremy the Younger creeping closer to us, nudging his playground ball with his feet. I turn away from Bree and motion at him to kick me the ball. When he does, I kick it back to him.

"Stop that, please," Bree says. "This is important."

Again, he kicks the ball, and I send it back to him.

"So is this."

Bree stomps across the floor to her brother and grabs him by the sleeve. He lets out a wail. As she drags him past me, he reaches out, and his fingers just barely touch my arm.

"You're it," he calls as she pulls him away.

CHAPTER 19

BE THE STRIPES

At morning kickstart, none of the snacks are appealing, and I am late anyway. I sit in my spot at the back of the room. Trace is late, too, and slips in next to me, eating a handful of rice crackers.

"These need ketchup," he says, trying to make me laugh.

"Ketchup has nine grams of sugar and red dye number 40," I whisper. Trace rolls his eyes.

The lights snap off, and Tully is standing on the stage in front of the glowing projection screen. Suddenly, an entire screen full of zebras appears.

"What do we have here?" Tully shouts.

A chorus of little kid voices shouts back, "Zebras!"

Stanley raises his hand and says, "A group of zebras is a zeal or a dazzle."

Tully gives him a double thumbs up. "And what else?"

Tiny Gemma says in her butterfly voice, "Stripes!"

Tully says in his serious voice, "Stripes. Yes, Gemma, stripes."

The screen flashes and now, instead of zebras, only the outlines appear. On each zebra, the stripes fill in to show that stripes aren't the same from zebra to zebra. I stop looking because it makes my head hurt. Tully keeps talking

"Zebras are very interesting creatures. Their stripes are completely original. No two alike. Those stripes make it hard to spot them in a forest because they blend into the background. When they stand together as a group, it's hard to tell where one zebra ends and another begins. They are a true representation of teamwork. They are strong and loyal to each other. They understand that they must take care of each individual to make the group strong. As you work through your second week at Equator School, think of yourself as a zebra, a unique individual. A member of a fortified team. Most importantly, don't just be the zebra. Be the stripes."

Walking to Chemistry with Trace, I hear Bree behind us.

"Now go out there and be the best darn zebra you can be!"

Trace whips around and, walking backward as natural as walking forward, folds his arms and smiles at her.

"Hey Bree, what did the blond name her pet zebra?"

Bree sticks out her tongue at him.

"Spot!" Trace spins on his heels, moonwalks, and ducks into Chemistry as David, Ben and I laugh behind him.

Trace and I sit together in Chemistry. He isn't a top student. He gets Cs and Ds like me and even got an F in History once. He is so happy all the time that I wonder how can he really be a seventh-grader at a school for kids who have messed up everything. That's what I've decided Equator School is. A school for kids who fail at school. Trace almost never stops talking, reciting poetry or singing. And what I can't figure out is why he isn't the least bit embarrassed to be seen with me.

We learn a new way to remember the Periodic Table of the Elements. Mrs. Yaw gives us twenty minutes to play Elemental War while she floats around the room making sure everyone is doing something reasonably close to studying. Trace has a set of elemental flash cards. He shuffles them and deals me twenty. The object of the game is to make the most words out of your cards.

Trace comes up with NoONe. I get BaSIC. We go back and forth putting words together. I get CaNDY, FIRe, and FLaSH. Trace gets KNIFe, BArF, and AmEriCan. We keep going until Mrs. Yaw calls time, then we make a list of our words and quiz each other on properties of the elements in each word we made. By the end of class, I know the properties of Calcium, Ruthenium, Iron and at least twenty others.

I feel sick when it's time for fourth period in Room 3.14. I almost hide out in the bathroom, but Trace pulls me along when I hang behind.

Tully explains that we are a team and a team needs a leader. The class captain's job is to lead the class in daily warm-ups, assist Tully with teaching new moves, and supervising small group work, like when we break off to work in teams. He asks for nominations.

Hazel's hand shoots up. "I nominate Trace."

She is shooting a fierce look at Bree, who looks daggers back at her. Trace cartwheels to the front of the group then bows theatrically. Hazel and I clap for him. It's strangely still, and Trace looks uncertain. I look up and down the beam. Everyone, except Hazel, is looking at the floor. Not Bree. She is swinging her legs seated on the beam, blowing a bubble with her gum and looking not the least bit worried.

"Any other nominations? Last call."

A hand goes up slowly next to me. It's Joey, who is a fourth grader.

"Bree," he says quietly.

Now I see it. Joey looks positively terrified even speaking her name. Bree leaps off the beam and stands next to Trace, throwing her arm around his shoulders and popping a bubble at him.

"Let's do this," she says enthusiastically.

"Great!" Says Tully. "Let's hear from each of our nominees, why should we vote for you for class captain? Trace, would you like to go first?"

"Three words," Trace begins. "Safety. I'll make sure everyone knows and follows safe Parkour practice." Hazel and I clap, and Bree looks at us coldly.

"Teamwork," Trace continues. "We'll all share responsibility for the setup and tear down and tidying up the gym." A few kids groan at that one.

"Uh, and finally, respect. If I am class captain, everyone will be treated with respect. That is all. Vote for me." He takes a bow and Hazel and I clap loudly. The rest of the group claps solemnly. Hazel shoots me a look that says, something is up.

Bree claps for Trace. "Gosh, I think that's a great list if you are running for King of the Nobodies. When I am class captain, I will personally assure that this will be a year of surprises and rewards and fun. Oh, and cupcakes. Vote for me, and you won't regret it."

She signals to Joey, who comes out from behind the wall with a tray full of, yep, cupcakes.

"These cupcakes are definitely not gluten, sugar or food color free. Enjoy!"

Tully moves to intercept the cupcakes, but half the kids are already licking the frosting off the tops, so he stops and shakes his head. Then he calls for a vote. She wins, of course. Only Hazel, me and another seventh grader named Karmen, who almost never speaks, vote for Trace.

Trace, Hazel, Karmen and I huddle together after class, while Bree walks around triumphantly telling everyone what she wants them to practice at home.

"Did Bree say something to you?" Hazel asks Karmen. Karmen pulls a note from her pocket and slips it to Hazel. Hazel reads it out loud.

"I know what you did, and I'm telling your mom. Vote for me for class captain tomorrow, or you will regret it!" It had a drawing of a person with creepy wide empty circles for eyes. Hazel hands the note back to Karmen.

"Funny, that's exactly what my note said. Jeremy, did you get a note?" Hazel asks.

"Sort of."

Trace, for the first time, looks like the happy has drained out of him.

CHAPTER 20

FAKED OUT

We walk to the pickup lane together. Trace is quiet with his hands shoved in his pockets. Hazel chatters angrily. Karmen still hasn't said a word.

"I can't believe she scared everyone else into voting for her! I'm going to tell Tully and show him the notes she gave us," Hazel fumes.

Karmen speaks up. "No, don't. She'll do something awful to me. She's already going to tell my mom."

"Tell her what? She can't know that much about you!" Hazel exclaims. She turns to Trace. "We're new here, but you're not. How could Bree possibly know stuff about us already? Is it written down somewhere?"

Trace shakes his head. "I don't know, I guess they must have files on us. I know my file has all my report cards and tests from the doctor and notes from all the conferences I have with Tully and Nugent. Nugent keeps all that stuff in her office."

I think of the Folder of Failure and wonder if everyone's mom keeps a folder full of their worst moments? Just then Tully's voice booms across the sidewalk.

"Jeremy! There you are. Hey, Trace, that was a good campaign speech you gave today. You handled it like a champ."

"Thanks," Trace says gloomily.

"Jeremy," Tully says, "I have a message from your mom. She's not able to pick you up today. Your dad will be here instead." When I hear the rumble of the diesel engine, Trace, Hazel and Karmen, disappear in the background. I forget everything except how much I've missed that sound.

A lot of things are different about my dad, but I notice first that he has a beard. We go to Dave's Burger Joint, and he buys me a vanilla milkshake and a plain burger with ketchup only. Dad gets himself an iced coffee, and we sit by the tree house, but I don't go climbing. I've wished for him to come back every day and I don't want to watch him from up there. I want to be with him. Dad looks at me across the table, but his eyes don't stay in one spot for very long.

"How's the new school?"

"It's okay."

"Just okay? Were those your friends?"

"I guess."

That's all he says for a long time. His eyes dart around, checking out everyone who walks in and every car that passes. There's a question I want to ask, but I'm afraid of the answer.

"You wanna go play?" He points up at the tree house. I shake my head. Now I am afraid that if I leave the table, he will disappear. He already seems to be not here.

"Dad," I say, "Are you coming home?" I brace for the no, but he doesn't answer. His hands are shaky. He glances around the room. He pulls a coffee stirrer out of a thin plastic wrapper and sticks it in his mouth.

"Dad?"

"Baby steps," he says. "Your mom has a new job. Couldn't make it to pick-up."

"Will you be picking me up every day?" He doesn't answer that question either.

"You sure you don't feel like playing on the monkey bars or something? We can go to the park if you want."

He knows I hate the park. There's nothing to do there. It's a big empty grass field, and the playground is full of sand and ants. I hate the feeling of sand in my shoes. Plus, I feel stupid because no one talks to me. Going to the park is like walking into a birthday party you weren't invited to.

He sips his coffee and chews on the plastic stirrer and doesn't say anything else. When we get in his truck to leave, I notice that the bed is full of stuff. Garbage bags tied shut, a sleeping bag and some dirty pillows.

"This was nice," he says when we stop in front of the apartment. Mom's car isn't in the parking space in front of our stairs. I suddenly feel panicked. He's going to leave again, and I don't know how to find him.

"Dad," I say, then I burst into tears. "Please don't leave."

Dad hugs me but doesn't say what I want to hear. Even worse, he says nothing at all. When Mom pulls up alongside the truck, I'm panic-stricken, and I grab his arm.

"Come inside. Come inside and see my room."

"Jeremy, I can't."

"Please, Dad, come in."

Mom opens her car door, and I cling to his arm. She stands outside the truck window and watches. Dad pushes me away.

"Stop that, now, Jeremy. We had a nice time."

I stop. It wasn't a nice time. It was a big fake-out. It was a trick. I climb out of the truck and run upstairs. I hear the diesel rumble as he pulls away. I push past Mom and run up to my bedroom. I want to throw something, but there isn't much to throw. I am suddenly aware how empty our apartment is. I have a bed and some clothes. A backpack and shoes. A pillow and a blanket. A bunch of stupid baby games. That's all I have. I used to have more.

I lock my bedroom door, crawl into bed, scrunch up my pillow and curl into the tightest ball I can. Close the lid. But my brain won't stop talking. I'm in my box, but all the noise has followed me in.

There are no safe places to hide anymore.

Chapter 21

Obstacles

Bree has everyone lined up doing gorilla walks from one side of the gym to the other. Tully walks in right behind me and slaps me on the back.

"Quadrupedal gallops! Great exercise," he says to the room.

Then to me, "Jeremy, let's have a talk."

We go to Tully's office, which is right down the hall from Room 3.14. Tully offers the choice of a large yoga ball or a chair. I choose the chair, and he takes the yoga ball.

"I like to check in with all of our new students now and then. How do you like Parkour?"

"I like it."

"I think it's a good fit for you. What do you like about it?"

"I don't know. I just like it."

Tully nods. "Have you solved the Rubik's Cube yet?"

I shake my head. "Stanley is really close."

"Actually, he solved it this morning."

I smile a little. Good for Stanley.

"Jeremy, I can't help but notice you seem down today. I'm wondering if there is something we should talk about."

This is a weird conversation. I think he is fishing for

something, but I don't know what. I don't answer for a long time.

"No. I'm tired."

"Okay. If you change your mind, I'm always here for you. You can talk to Dr. Nugent or me anytime."

He is bouncing up and down on the yoga ball.

"I have a job for you. I like to choose a new student every day to be the greeter at the door of the MPR for morning kickstart. It's a great way to get to know some meet the other students and practice some of the skills you've been learning."

"Parkour skills?"

"Making eye contact. Learning names. Showing interest in conversations. Stuff like that."

"Ah," I nod. "Yeah, no thanks. I don't like any of those things."

"Tomorrow it is!" Tully declares, nearly falling off the yoga ball. "Let's go do some Parkour."

Back in the gym, Tully calls everyone together. "Folks, gather around, I have an important announcement."

Trace nudges me. "What'd he talk to you about?"

"I have to be at the door of the MPR tomorrow morning."

"Oh, that. You're the doorstop," Trace says. "When I was the doorstop, I wore my horse head mask from Halloween." He cups his hand around his mouth, "You should wear something like a Fedora or a bow tie."

"Tully wears a bow tie."

"Exactly!"

Tully stands up on a beam. "Listen up! Every year, one student from the entire school wins a valuable prize. This prize is a scholarship to a summer camp of your choosing."

Bree whispers, "Will Hazel go to fat camp?"

Hazel curls her fingers into a fist, but Trace puts a hand on her arm and shakes his head.

He names the all-expenses-paid summer camp options. There's Parkour camp, drama camp, art camp, engineering camp, math camp, and space camp. One person out of the whole school gets their camp for free.

Hazel raises her hand. "How does someone win?"

"Thank you for asking, Hazel. The teaching staff, myself and Dr. Nugent will select a winner. The contest is based on three criteria. One, dedication to improvement. Two, teamwork. And the third is your why. Not why do you want to win, but the why that makes you who you are."

Truth Number Five. I've already lost.

"Take it away, Captain," Tully says and steps back.

"Okay, Zebras, gather around!" Bree calls out. Tully nods in approval as she describes an obstacle course, our first real Parkour run, laid out in front of us.

"First, it's a set of three balance beams—low, middle and high—chose your vault over each one. Next is a horizontal bar. Get a run at it, leap and grab the bar with both hands and swing. You're going to make a bar-to-wall jump, also called a cat leap. Pull up on top of the wall, and you'll see the foam pit in front of you and a rope ladder a few feet ahead of you. Jump to the rope ladder. Make sure you grab hold of the top knot and position your feet on the bottom knot. Any questions so far?"

Hazel raises her hand. Bree ignores her and continues.

"Swing over the foam pit to the other side without falling in. Let's go!"

"Here we go, zebras!" Shouts Tully from the other side of the course. He is running a timer. "This is what we've been training for, your first real Parkour course!"

Trace goes first. He clears the beams with a perfect speed vault. He sprints to the horizontal bar, pumps his legs up and swings so high, Karmen and Hazel both gasp because he looks like he'll swing over the top. He releases the bar and flies at the wall, his feet and fingers hitting at the same time. Gripping the top edge of the wall with his fingertips, Trace takes two steps, literally walking up the wall and standing up on top. On the other side of the wall, he leaps for the rope. His fingers slip, and he drops down into the pool of foam blocks.

A groan rises from the group. Everyone knows that climbing out of the foam pit is like trying to run underwater.

But Trace doesn't stop. He climbs out and up to the platform, lunges for the rope and this time swings all the way across the foam pit and lands on the other side. We all clap and cheer.

"Great first run! And, nice recovery," Tully says, calling Trace's time at 1:45. Trace is sweating, and his face is red when he jogs back to the line.

Bree goes next. She flies through the course like it is a walk down the hall. Her time almost half of Trace's time, most of which he lost in the foam pit.

"This can't possibly be as easy as you two make it look," Hazel says. "I don't think I can do this."

"Sure, you can," Trace says. "Look, the trickiest part is sticking to the wall. It looks far away from the bar when you start swinging, but it's not. When you're in the swing, and you see the top of the wall straight ahead, that's the time to let go. If you don't think you can make it take an extra swing. Bring your arms down and your knees up, like you are sitting in a chair. Then use your toes and fingers to grip the wall at the same time. Remember to use your legs to push your body up, not your arms to pull it."

When it's my turn to run, I go over the beams with a lazy vault. I miss my jump at the horizontal bar the first time. I pump my legs hard, and when I release the bar, the wall is just a few feet away. I grab the edge, use my feet to push up on top of it. I'm happy for the grip on my shoes. When I get to the foam pit, I capture the rope on the first try and make a decent landing on the other side. My time: 1:16 seconds.

At the end of the class, Bree wins the course run easily. My second run is slower than my first by ten seconds. Hazel takes a slip on the wall and falls back down on the floor. After three tries she barely makes it, scraping her knees and her hands. On her third attempt, she makes it to the rope swing but slips into the pit.

At the end of class, everyone gets a high five from Tully.

Hazel's face is red, and she looks ready to cry as we leave the gym. I tell her that it's no big deal. But Bree lingers at the door, and her eyes are pinned on Hazel.

CHAPTER 22

FAULT

Bree holds the door open for Hazel and whispers something to Hazel that I can't hear.

Hazel doesn't hesitate. She slaps Bree across the face. Bree smacks her face back and pushes her across the hall up against the wall. She hits Hazel in the stomach and Hazel doubles over and sinks to the floor.

"Woah! Woah!" hollers Tully, racing across the gym. "Stop!"

Trace and I run to help Hazel up off the floor while Tully holds Bree back.

"Go on to lunch, now, everything is okay," Tully says to the gathering crowd. Tully takes Bree and Hazel down the hall to Dr. Nugent's office and closes the door behind them.

"What just happened?" Karmen gasps.

Trace says, "I'm not sure."

"Did you see who started it?"

"Bree said something, then Hazel slapped her."

Karmen looks at me. "Did you hear anything?"

"I'm not even sure what I saw."

No one sees Hazel or Bree again until parent pick-up. Hazel's face is red, and her eyes are watery. Bree has a red splotch across her face and looks happier than ever.

"She thinks she can bully me," Hazel says. "Now, I'm on probation. Both of us are. I took the first swing, so I am in the most trouble, with my mom, anyway." Hazel starts to cry. "We're both disqualified from the summer scholarship contest if there is another incident."

"What did she say to you?" Trace asks. Hazel just weeps. Her mom pulls up, and Karmen hugs Hazel before she gets in the car.

"Good luck," Karmen says. "I wish we could show everyone what kind of stripes that zebra has."

I feel Bree staring at me, and I sit down on the curb, put my head down on my knees and let my hair curtain do its job. Until I feel a little nudge. It's Dr. Nugent.

"Your mom is going to be late," she says in her always pleasant voice. "Follow me." Dr. Nugent leads me to her office.

"Go ahead and have a seat at the work table, Jeremy. You can spend some time on homework while you are waiting." Not a word about what happened today. I put my head down on the table and fall asleep. It's almost five when my mom comes. Dr. Nugent shakes me awake. I quickly wipe the slobber off the table with my shirt, embarrassed. She laughs.

"Don't worry about it Jeremy, I know how hard you are trying. It's exhausting."

Tully and Dr. Nugent both seem to think they know more about me than they really do. All I know is that I'm tired, but I can't sleep; I want to eat, but I can't eat; I want to sleep but I'm hungry, and everything seems impossible.

"Here, I have something to show you." She takes a paper off the top of her desk. "Your Chem quiz. You got an 85."

I check the name on the quiz before I believe her.

"That's a B, isn't it?"

"It's a solid B," she says with a smile. "You earned that nap." I take the quiz from her as my mom enters.

"I'm so sorry. I have a new job, and it's hard to get away to pick-up on time. We need a new plan." She's stressed. I know the stressed look. Her hair is messy, and she talks too fast. Dr. Nugent asks me to wait in the hall while she talks to mom.

"Hey," Mom says, as we walk to the car. "Dr. Nugent said you got a B on a chemistry quiz. You want to go to Dave's to celebrate?"

"No," I say sharply. Mom looks surprised.

"Okay. You choose, then."

"I just want to go home."

Mom sighs. "Jeremy, we have some things to talk over. Let's order a pizza, okay?"

"Whatever." I turn to the window and close my eyes. I should be happy. I got a B on a test in a subject I've never even had before. I did my first Parkour course and didn't completely blow that either.

While we wait for the pizza to show up, Mom sits down across the table from me.

"Listen, I wanted to tell you that I got a raise at my job and it's going to help us get a house again, someday. That's the good news. But I will need to work late one night a week, so on that day you are going to have to ride the city bus home."

I drop my head on the table. I have never even been on the inside of a bus. In fact, the only thing I know is that Gemma wants to bake a cake for the fictional homeless guy that sits at the bus stop all day. There isn't even a bus required for that scenario.

"It's easy, just one bus, then walk a couple of blocks home. After dinner, we'll drive the route, and I'll show you, okay?"

"No," I say stubbornly. "Not okay. I don't want to ride the bus."

"Jeremy, it's just once a week. It's a good thing for you to learn, so maybe when you want to visit your friends..."

"Why can't Dad pick me up?" I explode at her. "Why did you make him leave?"

The doorbell rings. Mom goes silent. She doesn't move to answer it, so I get up and take the pizza from the delivery man, slam the door to make a point that I am mad, then drop the pizza on the table in front of her. It's gluten-free crust anyway, which shouldn't even be allowed to be called pizza.

"I'm not riding the bus." I go into my room and slam that door, too, in case she missed the first one.

I don't sleep that night either. I feel awful. I hear my mom go to bed and after she is asleep, I get up and go to the fridge for pizza. She's already put it on a plate with a note that says, "I'm sorry, and I love you."

The truth is that she didn't make Dad leave. I did. I wore him out. I made everything harder than it had to be when I was picky about my clothes and shoes and stuff. I failed school. He lost jobs because I got in trouble and he had to come get me when Mom couldn't leave work. Every fight my mom and dad ever had was about me. Everything my dad got mad about was my fault. I didn't listen when he said he was tired and said I should wait until the weekend to try the experiment and I burned down our house. He sat on that rock and thought about all the awful things I did and that this was too much. It was the last thing I did wrong before he left for good. It wasn't my mom's fault he left. It was mine.

I wrote on Mom's note, "I'm sorry, too," with a sad face and a heart, and slid it under her door.

CHAPTER 23

MONE ME SI ERRO

Tully doesn't let me forget that I am the door stop today. He is waiting at drop off and escorts me to the door of the MPR. He even takes my pack for me and puts in on a seat in the front, where Trace and Hazel usually sit.

"Now, some kids like to call this being the doorstop," he says cheerfully. "I like to think of it as being the door start. You get to start off someone's day by being helpful. And that starts your day off splendidly!"

I position myself to hold the door open. It's a perfect opportunity for the hair curtain. Some kids just plow through and don't look at me. Others nod or say hello, and I mumble an unconvincing "good morning" back to them. A couple, mostly girls, say "Thank you." One little kid gives me a fist bump. Bree walks by without so much as a sneer, pushing her brother ahead of her even though he tries to hand me something. A few minutes later he runs back to me and hands me a note, which I shove in my pocket.

Everyone is buzzing with chatter about the girl fight yesterday. They want to see Hazel, who is sitting in the front row sliding down in her seat, clutching her backpack. Bree sits in front of her, not even trying to hide the purple bruise on her face. She's enjoying every minute of attention. Tully walks to the microphone and hushes the room. He motions to me that I can close the door and take my seat up front.

"Choices," Tully says. "Let's talk today about choices. You make hundreds of choices every day. Some choices are easy, and you're not even aware of them. Some choices are very hard. Today we want to be very aware of the importance of making good choices."

Bree looks in my direction and rolls her eyes.

Tully goes on. "On the paper in front of you, write down one choice that you made today. It can be anything. What you ate for breakfast. Which side you part your hair. Whether to get out of bed at the alarm, or hit the snooze button for another nine minutes. Which socks you wear. And, that, I know is a difficult choice."

I wear the same type of shorts and shirts every day because I chose them a long time ago and they work. It's only been this year that I agreed to add different colors of shirts if they are the same shirt, with a pocket on the front and the tag cut out. But I didn't give up my black nylon shorts with pockets and an elastic waistband.

"No matter how small that choice was, there was a reason you chose it. Write down why you made that choice. Then pass those papers face down to the end of the aisle for Dr. Nugent to collect, please."

Trace writes, "I chose to eat waffles with strawberry jam. Because awesome!"

Hazel writes, "I chose to be an idiot. Because I am one."

I hurriedly write down, "I chose not to answer. I don't know why."

Tully goes on. "Today, I would like each of you to be aware that almost everything you do involves a choice. Now, that's not encouragement to obsess over it for those of you prone to obsessing over choices," he pauses to smile at Stanley. "Don't let it freeze you up. The goal today is to be aware that you have great control over your day, all because of the choices you make."

Then Tully ends his lecture reminding everyone about the summer scholarship contest. But he changes something.

"Yesterday, we told you about a great opportunity to win our summer scholarship contest. Today, we are adding a twist. An added incentive. Every one of you will, at some point, rely on the help of one another to be successful, and you must make good choices to be successful. For the first time, the winner of the summer scholarship contest will get to choose another student to go along. Essentially, there will be two winners. So, remember teamwork. Remember kindness. Remember the five truths."

I'm watching Bree when he says this, and I swear, she looks worried. Then she looks down the table at me and smiles like she is my best friend. She holds up two fingers. Peace. I look away.

Walking to class, I ask Hazel, "So, what did Bree say to you before you smacked her?"

"Yes, what did she say that made you choose to hit her?" Trace asks.

Hazel doesn't answer. She glares at us and takes a detour to the girls' bathroom.

Trace says, "I think she is choosing not to talk about it."

I get nervous as the day goes on. This morning, Mom and I left early, and she drove me along the bus route. She gave me money for the fare, showed me where to get on the bus and where to get out at 52nd Street and Maple Avenue. We live in Maple Grove Apartments, two blocks from the intersection of 52nd Street and Maple Avenue. She writes our address, her name and work phone number down on a green sheet of paper, which I put in the outside pocket of my backpack. She gives me my own key to the apartment. I am supposed to call her when I get home.

Written on that one piece of paper is more than I have ever known about where I live. I knew every inch of my house from dirt to rooftop. I bet I could pick it out of the sky from an airplane. But I couldn't tell you what street I lived on or the house number or how to get there from school.

Dr. Nugent meets me at my locker at the end of the day.

"Hi Jeremy, can you walk with me for a minute? How did your day go?"

"Okay."

"I heard that you had a Latin quiz today. How do you feel you did?"

"Mone me si erro," I reply.

She laughs her happy laugh, the one I remember from preschool. "Excellent! Of course, I will. In fact," she pauses to push open the front door of the school, "I'm making sure you get to your bus stop okay."

"I have it all written down," I say, swinging my backpack around to take out the paper Mom gave me. I shuffle around all the others in my pack, but it's not there. She even wrote it on green paper so I could find it easily.

"I have to go back, I lost the directions. I need to check my locker."

"The bus arrives in nine minutes, hurry, okay? I'll wait for you here at the front."

I race up the hall to my locker and rummage through the notebooks, but there is no green paper. My head feels dizzy, and my face is sweaty. It's the way I feel when I panic. I run to every classroom I was in today, look in trashcans, even check Room 3.14 and the boys' bathroom, but no green paper.

I'm out of breath when I get back to Dr. Nugent.

"I can't find it, the paper that tells me how to get home. I have to find it."

"Okay, we'll figure it out," Dr. Nugent says. "The bus comes again in 25 minutes. Let's call your Mom at work and let her know you are okay." She calls the number, but someone tells her my mom is busy and can't take any calls now.

"I have your address, Jeremy. Let's figure this out. No need to panic, okay?"

She gets on the phone again while I go to the drinking fountain. When I look out the window, I see Bree standing outside in the parent pickup lane. Then I see Jeremy the Younger. He's tossing something in the air and chasing it. Something green. A green paper airplane.

"Hey, that's mine!" I holler. But Bree doesn't hear, and she gets in the car with her brother before I can run outside and stop her.

Now I'm not just panicked, I'm angry. How did she get it out of my backpack? How did she even know it was important? I go over the day in my head. My mom dropped me off. She gave me the paper. I put it in my pack. I had my pack with me all day.

Except at morning kickstart when Tully put my pack on a seat for me. She sat down next to my pack while I was at the door. After that, she gave me a smile and a peace sign.

Dr. Nugent walks out of her office and hands me another note. "Here you are," she says. "Let's get you to the bus stop, okay?"

The bus stop is a few minutes' walk from the school. Dr. Nugent waits with me until the bus comes.

"Get your bus fare ready, and you'll put it into a fare machine when you board the bus. You've got this," she says. When the bus pulls up, she walks me to the door and waves at the driver as I step on.

"It's his first time, can you help him if he needs it?"

The driver looks at her and says in a gruff voice, "Sure, sweetheart."

Dr. Nugent walks away as the doors squeak closed. *Mone me si erro*, I think, as the bus driver looks me up and down.

Warn me if I wander.

CHAPTER 24

CHOICES

When the bus door closes, my head buzzes. I can't think of what to do next. The driver has a shaggy beard like my dad's. He glares at me when I hand him my fare. I try to say the name of the street where I need to get off, but the bus screeches back onto the road. I sway to the side and grab a bar to steady myself.

"In the box." He points to a metal column with a digital display that counts down the coins as I drop them in. "Now sit."

I feel eyes follow me as I walk down the aisle. I look for an empty seat and end up at the back of the bus. I am calm walking along the edge of a roof, why should I be terrified on a bus? But I am. I watch out the window for my street. Nothing looks familiar, and suddenly, I have trouble breathing, and everything spins. I stand up and make my way to the front.

Don't be an idiot, I tell myself. It's just a stupid bus. I hold onto the metal bar by the driver's seat as he stops to pick up more passengers.

"Excuse me." I show him the paper from Dr. Nugent. "I need to get off at Maple."

He points to a cord that I hadn't noticed before. It runs

along the top of the windows. "Three more miles. Pull the cord when you want to exit the bus."

The bus lurches and screeches as I walk back to my seat, feeling sicker with every turn. I try to remember how far a mile is. I hug my backpack in my lap and watch out the window for anything familiar, but even though Mom drove through the route, I'm too nervous to remember. I read Dr. Nugent's note, which says the bus will make seven stops before it gets to Maple Street. But I haven't been counting the stops. I never hear the driver call out Maple Street like Mom said he would so that I can pull the cord. He never calls out anything. He doesn't even look back to see if I am still alive. I fish into my pocket for something to fidget with, and I find the note Jeremy the Younger gave me this morning. I'd forgotten about it. I read it, crumple it up and leave it on the seat.

I need to get off the bus now, or I am going to barf. It feels like I've been on it forever. I'm sweating and shaking as I reach for the cord. The bus keeps moving to the next stop where I get off and stand on the street corner, squinting in the bright sun to read the name of the street.

It's not Maple Street. It's Washington Street. The only store I recognize is a C-Stop. I cross two streets to get to it. I go inside and ask to use the bathroom. The clerk gives me a key that is attached to a stick of wood. I barely make it before I throw up in the sink. I stay in there until someone is tapping on the door. It's the clerk. I unlock the door, and he asks if I am okay.

I don't answer. I can't answer. I'm not okay.

"Kid, can I call someone for you?"

I hand him the paper from Dr. Nugent.

When Mom arrives, she hugs me and waves to the clerk who waves back at her.

"How did you end up here?" Her voice is shaking, and she is in terrified mode. "What happened?"

My voice finally comes back, but I cry like a little kid. In between sobs, I tell her that I couldn't see the streets and the bus driver never called the stops out, so I didn't know where I was. We aren't even home, and she is already on the phone with the city bus people, crying and yelling.

"Your driver left a 12-year-old kid on South Washington Street. Two miles away from where he needed to get out!" She hollers into the phone. "A child riding the bus for the first time because I have to be at work."

I plug my ears until she stops yelling. Now she is telling the story to a new person.

"You think I wanted to send him home on the city bus? I have no other choice. I can't afford after-school care, I can barely pay for the school he needs."

"It costs money to go there?" I'm surprised. She shushes me.

"Equator School. Yes. How did you know? That sounds a lot like him."

When we get to the apartment, she goes into her room and closes the door to finish talking on the phone. When she comes out of her room, I am asleep on the floor in front of the TV, and she nudges me awake.

"I'm so sorry. I never dreamed it would be such a mess riding the bus."

"It's not your fault," I say. Most things are not her fault, but she always apologizes for them. This was all me. Bree stole the instructions. I panicked. I can't remember things. My mind seizes up like a fist, and I can't do anything.

"How much does school cost?" I ask.

"I don't want you worrying about that," she says. "The school gave you a scholarship, and I pay a little each month. I don't have enough for the after-school program. Maybe next year. But for now, until my work schedule changes, you'll have to ride the bus on Wednesdays."

"Please, I'd rather walk," I beg. "Please don't make me ride the bus."

"Next week, someone from the bus company will be there to help you. Her name is Marie, and she knows all about Equator School. I talked to her on the phone, and she promised to be there to show you how to get home safe. Just give it one more try, okay, please? I don't have a choice right now."

Choices again. I can think of a dozen ways I could get home that doesn't involve the bus. But Tully didn't say what to do when you have no choice.

CHAPTER 25

SECRETS

"I think Tully knows what he is doing," Hazel says. "Bree can't get too mean, or not only will she lose the summer scholarship contest, no one will choose her to go with them."

Trace disagrees. "It's going to force her to be sneakier. She's already scared most of the class into voting her captain. Now, she has to keep them scared so they'll stay quiet."

We're setting up a new obstacle course. Trace and I move around the huge blocks, while Hazel and Karmen position the beams. Almost everything in Room 3.14 is movable so we can set up a different course every week. I like to picture us as tiny mouse-sized people, pushing around a bunch of toy blocks. Ants on a leaf, thinking we are the whole world.

"We don't vote for the scholarship winner. The teachers do," Karmen says.

"That's right. But the winner gets to choose the other winner," Hazel says. "It could be anyone."

"She can't possibly get to everyone in the school, even the upper-grade kids, can she?" I ask.

Karmen looks up at the high bar that we'll soon be using to swing from one wall to an even higher wall and says, "Everyone is scared of something."

Normally I don't like math, but today, there's candy. All kinds of it. Chocolate drops, sours, jelly beans, gummy bears and peppermints, all separated into baggies and piled into a plastic tub on Mr. Carpenter's desk. There's also a measuring tape and clipboard on every desk. We get into groups of four, and Mr. Carpenter drops a baggie of candy-coated chocolate drops right on the table.

"Here you are, one bag of food coloring and benzene sulphonic acid treated with hydrochloric acid and sodium nitrite."

Trace groans. "You know we can't eat this stuff."

Mr. Carpenter winks at him. "We aren't eating it. We're calculating with it."

Hazel leans over from the table next to us. "I heard he's been using these same bags of candy for three years!"

"I don't care. It's candy," Trace says.

We calculate the volume of a cylinder and write it down on our clipboard. We figure out how many candies it takes to fill the cylinder. Mr. C. sends us to find a large area to measure and calculate how many candies would fit in the area. Some kids head to the library. Another group decides to measure a wall of lockers. Hazel, Karmen, Trace and I head to Room 3.14. We measure the foam pit, which is fourteen feet long and ten feet across. Trace dives headfirst into it and works his way to the bottom. I lower the measuring tape to him. Seven feet deep.

We head back to the classroom to finish our calculations and pass by the lockers on the way there. One of the lockers is covered in bright colored sticky notes.

"Wow," says Hazel. "I'm glad that's not my locker."

Karmen stops walking. "That's my locker." Every one of the sticky notes has the word Liar written on it.

"Bree!" Hazel exclaims. "She's going after Karmen because she didn't vote for her."

We help Karmen remove all the sticky notes and throw them away, but when she opens her locker, shredded paper falls out all over the floor.

"Do you think anyone saw this?" Trace asks as we scramble to pick up all the tiny shreds of paper.

"I think we got lucky," Hazel says. "The group measuring lockers went to the other hall."

"But why would she do this?" asks Trace.

Karmen responds. "Because she warned me she would."

"You can't let her get away with this. You have to tell Tully," Hazel insists.

Karmen shakes her head vigorously.

"Why not? She'll keep doing it. She'll do it to someone else," Hazel says.

Karmen sighs. "It doesn't matter."

"What?" Trace exclaims. "Of course, it matters. It's practically a crime!"

I study Karmen's face, and I recognize something. Her hair is falling over her eyes. She's hiding.

"It's not what Bree did," I say. "It's what she knows. Isn't it?"

Karmen doesn't answer.

"What does she know? You lied about something? Big deal!" Hazel says. "We've all lied about something."

"It's more than that. She knows something that no one else is supposed to know, right?" I ask.

Karmen nods again. Hazel lights up.

"She's gotten into our files. She's seen our why circles. Maybe she saw the choices papers, too. She's got intel on us and knows things that are private. And embarrassing. We have to tell Dr. Nugent and Tully."

"No, not yet, we need proof," Trace says. He looks at me. "She knows something about you, too, doesn't she?"

Hazel jumps in. "It doesn't matter what she knows, what matters is how she found it. I can't believe Dr. Nugent would be that careless to let Bree have access to our files."

Trace agrees. "No. Dr. Nugent wouldn't be careless. She scans all kinds of papers into her computer, then they get shredded. She shreds the confidential stuff herself. She has a paper shredder right there in her office. I know, because once I had to shred files while taking some time to think things over.

When you need some cooling off time, you can shred stuff in Dr. Nugent's office. It's very satisfying. You know who does that practically every week?"

"Bree?" Karmen gasps.

"No," Trace says. "Her brother. Jeremy the Younger."

I don't believe that Jeremy the Younger has a cruel thought in his head. But that note I left behind on the bus. It was a drawing of a burning house and a person standing in a window with round, empty eyes saying, *I know what you did.*

CHAPTER 26

ONE DROP OF WATER

A woman named Marie waits for me on Wednesday. She chats with Dr. Nugent and Tully like they are friends.

"So nice to see you. Tell Thomas congratulations," Dr. Nugent says. "Here's Jeremy! This is Marie, she works for the city bus."

I was hoping everyone had forgotten about the bus incident.

"Hi Jeremy, I brought you a couple things. Let's walk to the bus stop, okay?" Marie hands me a tote bag. Inside are a city bus map, a Sudoku puzzle book, a pen, a small notebook, a granola bar and a bottle of water.

"Stay hydrated," she cautions with a smile. We sit on the metal bench under the bus shelter. Marie shows me how to read the timetable to see when the buses come and go.

"About what happened last week," Marie says kindly, "That driver was a substitute, and he won't be driving this route again. The regular driver will be here today. Our drivers are expected to help passengers with their travel, and I am sorry that you had a bad experience."

"It's okay."

"This is where you wait. The driver will always stop when he sees someone at the bus shelter," she says, as a bus appears down the street.

"I know."

"Okay. How much is bus fare?"

"One dollar ten cents."

"That's right. But not for you. This is your bus pass. It's good for the whole year. You can use it as much as you want." I take the laminated card.

"Thanks," I reply, but it feels like telling someone thank you for breaking only one of your legs.

When the bus comes close, I see it's not the same driver. It's a man with dark hair and light brown skin with dark freckles. He smiles at me when I get on. I show him my bus pass, and he points to a scanner on top of the metal column.

"Just slide it across there, and when you hear it beep, you're all done."

The machine beeps. Marie says, "Freddy, this is Jeremy, he'll be riding home on Wednesday afternoons."

"Welcome aboard, son. You can sit right there by me if you want. I don't bite," says Freddy.

Marie and I sit up front, in one of the seats that says "Please reserve for disabled passengers". Marie notices me looking at that sign.

"It's okay. We encourage people who need a little more help using the bus to sit close to the driver so you can ask questions."

I look at Marie's shoes and hope she can read my mind. I want to tell her that I know what to do. I can pull a cord. I can read a sign. I get lost sometimes in my own brain, and I can't keep track of the other stuff happening around me. Every noise the bus makes pulls me in another direction, trying to figure out the source of every grinding, squeaking, clanking, screeching noise. Because, how else do you know if something is broken? When the bus makes a stop, a noisy screech makes me jumpy. Marie notices.

"Those are the brakes. They can be a little noisy, but they are okay. The bus gets serviced monthly to make sure everything works."

I relax a little now that I know what that noise is.

"There are seven stops from Equator School to Maple Street," Marie says. "Let's find something at every stop that you can recognize. You might want to write this down."

I dig out the pen and notepad from the tote bag. We're approaching a huge building, the Arizona Science Center. It's made of multilevel walls and steps, with an imposing angular shape like a rocket ready to blast off. Lots of people are at this bus shelter, which isn't brown like the others.

"It's yellow," I say, pointing.

"Good," Marie says. "Stop number one is the yellow bus shelter at the science center." I write it down.

At the next stop, I hear the slowing screech, and I look out the window for a landmark. We are under a pedestrian bridge that people use to get from the bus to the train.

"A bridge. That's stop number two."

Next, we take a left turn and stop at a marketplace with food vendors, tables, and people selling flowers and jewelry. I write down market for number three. Just past the market, the bus takes a right turn and stops in front of a parking garage, where eight people get on. That's stop number four.

Stop number five is across from Constitution Park, where the grass is always green because it has a golf course. It also has a Ferris wheel, a carousel, a lake with paddle boats, and a skate park. My dad took me there once.

Next, Freddy takes a left turn, and now we are on a street I know because that's the street Mom drives to school. We stop next to a flower shop.

"Roses," says a sign in the window of the shop. Roses are number six.

The next stop is a donut shop. I miss donuts.

"Stop number seven. Donuts I'll never eat again."

Marie laughs. "Great job, the stop after donuts is yours." We arrive at 52nd Street and Maple. "Time to pull the cord."

When we get off the bus, Freddy says goodbye, and I decide he's a good guy because he smiles a lot and says hello to everyone. Marie and I walk to the corner and cross at the light.

"Hey, how about a Hawaiian shaved ice?" she offers. "Will your mom mind?"

Probably, but maybe not. I never knew there was a Hawaiian shaved ice shop right by the apartment. The problem with Hawaiian shaved ice is that there is an infinite number of syrup flavors and combinations. Marie is very patient while I decide on lime. It's the only food-coloring-free flavor.

We sit at the table in the tiny shaved ice store that has a noisy air conditioner over the doorway. It hums, gurgles and clanks while I try to listen to Marie, but the noise takes over. I remember being on the roof of my house and its old air conditioning unit that Dad was always fixing. He let me climb up and help him. I handed him tools from the toolbox and held the screws and nuts and bolts, so they didn't roll away. We tinkered with it until the clanking stopped and a steady hum took its place. Now, that was guy time.

"You are going to do fine, you know. My son, Thomas, graduated from Equator. It changed his life." Marie shows me a picture of Thomas. He's a skinny kid with glasses and long dark hair that falls over his eyes. In the picture, he's wearing a lab coat and holding a beaker with blue liquid in it.

"That was at science camp in sixth grade. Thomas loves chemistry. He knows everything there is to know about the periodic table," she says, proudly.

"Did he learn the game where you make words from the symbols?"

"Yes!" She laughs. "Also, he was Elemental Jeopardy winner. Have you played that game yet? It's like the game show Jeopardy, only the questions are all about the elements and science."

Marie shows me another picture. It's Thomas all grown up. His hair is trimmed above his ears and eyes, and he is wearing a dress shirt and tie.

"That's his college graduation," she says. "You know, I was telling your mom, Thomas is a lot like you. He failed sixth grade and barely squeaked by seventh grade. He is very smart but has a hard time focusing. Except when it is something he really loves, then you can't get him to stop focusing on it. It always seemed like he was somewhere else inside his head. But now he works as a chemist researching drugs to cure cancer."

I look at the picture of Thomas. I can't imagine being like me and doing something so important like helping cure cancer.

"Thomas hated school until I moved him to Equator. Regular schools didn't understand that even though he is smart, he has a lot of anxiety and doesn't learn the same way most kids learn. He needs more time to think because his brain works differently. You understand that, don't you?" Marie asks.

"School's not my favorite thing, either."

"Your mom did a really good thing, you know," Marie says, noisily slurping the last of her shaved ice through a straw. I do the same, and we both laugh.

"What do you mean?"

"She saw that she couldn't do it by herself. I bet she tells you every day that you are a great kid and she loves you."

Now I feel sad because it's true. She does. Sometimes I hear her say stuff like that while standing in my doorway at night checking on me when she thinks I'm asleep.

"She knows she can't do it alone. She found other people, like Dr. Nugent and Tully, to help her. They understand how your brain works. They see all those good things in you. Maybe one day, you'll see them, too."

I stab the bottom of the cup with my straw. It feels weird for someone I barely know to be talking about me and my mom like she knows all about us. At the same time, it feels good to hear someone who isn't my mom saying nice things about me.

"Now, let's do a quick review before I walk you home. Can you remember the stops?"

I know this.

"Yellow shelter. Pedestrian bridge. Market. Parking garage. Park. Roses. Donut shop and Hawaiian ice!"

When we walk out of the Hawaiian ice store a drop of cold water from the air conditioning unit falls on my head, and I realize that I had gotten so interested in what Marie was saying, I forgot about the noise. But somewhere in my brain, I remember being on the roof with my dad, listening to every sound, watching his every move as he cleaned the copper coils of the noisy old unit. One thing you must have to survive a summer in Phoenix in air conditioning.

I turn around and walk to the counter. The man is reading a magazine. He looks up at me, and I tell him, "It's probably the condensate line. It's easy to fix yourself."

He sits the magazine down on the counter. "You know this how?"

I answer as if I had known it forever. "I can hear it."

He smiles and hands me a little coupon for a free ice. "Come back again for one on me," he says.

Marie walks me to the door. For the first time, I don't feel like I did something stupid by getting lost in my head. It isn't only noise, all that stuff knocking around inside. Every sound is a clue. And my brain doesn't want to miss any of it because you never know when you might need to fix something.

CHAPTER 27

BACKGROUND NOISE

Tully goes over the why circles. Again, we get a piece of paper. Again, we are asked to write down the reason why we are here. Does it change every week? I leave my circle empty. Tully walks by and peeks at my paper to see if I have written an answer. Sometimes he'll congratulate me on a good test score or something else I did. But when I hand in an empty circle, he never says a word.

Not until I have my private meeting with Tully does he ask me about the circles. When he does, he pulls out a file folder that has my name on it. Inside the file folder is every Why circle paper I have handed in. All of them are blank.

"Do you keep all of those, for everyone?" I ask.

"Yes," he says. "It helps a student see their progress."

"Here? In your office?"

"They get scanned into our secure file system and then shredded. These haven't been scanned yet, but they will soon." He changes the subject. "Jeremy, what's the hardest part of school for you?"

"All of it."

"You seem to be struggling in History. Five missed

assignments. That's tough to bounce back from. How can I help?"

"I don't know." I almost always answer Tully's questions with I don't know. He keeps talking anyway.

"You did an incredible job on your ancient habitats project. You must like to build things."

"I guess."

Tully picks up a Rubik's Cube twists it around. "You know, I've never solved this. Have you, yet?"

I shake my head. I kind of forgot about it after the first couple of weeks, when Stanley had solved his.

"I wonder, what makes a Rubik's Cube puzzle hard for you to solve, but you can build an almost perfectly proportioned, multi-level dwelling stabilized with support beams out of clay and a paper clip?"

"I don't know." Really, I don't.

"There are tricks to this cube that I never can remember. It sure is hard to put down, though," Tully says. "Hey, do you like Minecraft?"

Tully leads me to a room I've never noticed before. The door has no window, and it is painted the same color as the wall, with no handle on the outside, just a lock. He knocks three times, then waits, knocks two times, then waits, then one time. The door swings open. It's Turnbull.

"Hail, Jeremy! I knew you'd come eventually," he says jovially. "Come in, welcome to the Sandbox!"

Tully leaves me with a clap on the shoulder.

"Turnbull will brief you on the rules."

"Everyone, say hello to Jeremy! He's joining us for History. Let's see, Jeremy, have a seat next to Ben over there, and he'll help you get started."

I cannot believe this is happening. I am in a darkened classroom, with a laptop computer at every seat, headsets, and a bunch of kids I already know. Trace, Ben, and David are here. Jeremy the Younger is here. Bree is here. There are more kids I can't really see because they are in the dark with just the screen glow making their faces look menacing. This has got to be a dream. No school has a secret Minecraft classroom.

But it's real.

Ben points to the screen. "Choose a screen name or use your real name. I'm BenLordValor. David is MonkeeZombee. Trace is WithoutATrace. There's tutorial world, but if you've played before you don't need it. It's just like real Minecraft."

"Are you kidding me?" I am still in disbelief.

"You must take the pledge of the Sandbox," Turnbull says, standing behind me. "Trace, please explain."

"No one speaks of the Sandbox outside of the room. Don't show anyone on the outside the secret knock," Trace says.

"Ben, tell Jeremy the secret knock," Turnbull says.

Ben leans over and whispers, "There is no secret knock. Just knock in some random pattern, and we'll open the door."

David whispers, "We talk about it all the time, too. Just not with non-Sandboxers."

Sandboxers. I laugh and put on my headphones. There is music playing already. Minecraft music. No words, just instruments and sound. The music is what the stars might sound like if you could hear them. Chimes, calling birds, croaking frogs, chirping crickets, guitar, flutes, and falling rain.

I listen while I tap my fingers on the keypad. Then I have it. My new Minecraft screen name. It sounds right and feels right, like when you slip on your favorite pair of shoes that fit you perfectly.

BackgroundNoise.

CHAPTER 28

THE BARN

The barn course is the newest part of the Parkour gym, built by the Engineering Club. For the entire month, the whole gym is transformed into an Old West course which will be our final exam for the semester. The whole school is doing a Southwest Studies unit because we live in Arizona. In History, we learn about the Grand Canyon through a virtual tour we designed in Minecraft. It takes you through the canyon in a mining cart. You see how the early Native Americans lived, what they ate, and the wildlife that populated the canyon. We also learn how the Colorado River and the Grand Canyon have transformed because of humans using it for vacations. In Chemistry, we learn about elements mined in the Southwest, like copper and iron. Every day we get a new rock specimen to identify. We use chisels, picks and microscopes to figure out what kind of rocks we have.

The Engineering Club didn't build the Old West course by themselves. All the math classes helped. We took the measurements and wrote the specifications for the plans. We made sure every wall, beam, and block was placed in exactly the right spot, then we gave all the measurements to the Engineering Club, and they drew up a blueprint. A couple of weekends of work with dads who brought in tools and our Old West course was complete. Everyone who worked on the course got to sign their names on the blueprint, which now hangs in a frame on the wall outside of Room 3.14.

The barn itself is a fourteen-foot-tall square structure that looks like a house with windows for underbars. There's no door because Parkour doesn't need doors when it has windows. The barn is fifteen feet tall and lines right up with the foam pit. The rope to cross the foam pit has been replaced by a horizontal bar, which means you have to make a huge jump, grab the bar and swing all the way to the top of the barn. Fortunately, the engineers added a very bouncy trampoline to get momentum when you jump for the horizontal bar. Once on the barn, a roof is made of two beams that run from one side to the other. On the mat below, in front of the bar, is a hitching post to vault over.

The entire course is laid out in a square. It starts at suicide lanes that take you to the next move: a vault over a large buffalo. It's a foam block draped in a brown robe we got from Tully and a buffalo face drawn onto a paper plate. After you get over the buffalo, you cat-hang or walk up a wall to the trampoline that lines up with the foam pit. You leap, grab the bar and swing all the way to the roof. Criss-cross jump the beams to the front side of the barn, then leap to the mat below into a safety roll. Pop up, and you're at the hitching post. When you vault over the hitching post, you have to step across a watering hole full of killer non-native crawdads (a bunch of golf balls rolling around) without touching any. You're almost done. One more wall to clear however you choose. It's only five feet tall. That's like jumping off my head.

On the other side of the five-foot wall, you land in a scorpion-filled desert. Without touching a scorpion (represented by everyone's stinky shoes scattered across the mat), you must vault over three foam blocks. A camel awaits you on the other side of the last foam block. It's not very big, more like a medium-sized dog. Your task is to get the camel back to the barn. The catch is that you must reach the barn and secure the camel inside without being hit by Bree firing at you with a foam dart gun. That part is all her idea.

"A burro would be more appropriate to the natural fauna of the Southwest, or perhaps a bighorn sheep," Karmen comments. Tully explains that when he won a prize for throwing darts at balloons at the State Fair, he had his choice of a camel or Elmo.

Bree rolls her eyes and makes Karmen go first.

Ever since Bree littered Karmen's locker with "Liar" notes, we've watched closely for her next target and for clues to how she was getting secret information on us. Bree has daily check-ins with Dr. Nugent before and after school. But we haven't been able to catch her in the act. In fact, she's been on best behavior for quite a while. Because of their fight, both Hazel and Bree are required to check in with Dr. Nugent and show signatures from every teacher to verify they are following rules, turning in homework, participating in class and not fighting. I'm glad that isn't me. But I am glad that it's Hazel because she's a good snoop.

"Dr. Nugent has tons of files, but she scans everything into her computer, then shreds the originals, just like Tully said," Hazel tells us while we wait for our turn at the Old West course.

Trace asks, "Last year I got in a little trouble and had to be an office assistant after school for a month. I wonder if Bree gets office duty."

Hazel laughs. "What could you have possibly done wrong, Mr. Perfect?"

Trace looks embarrassed. "I kind of set a fire in my locker."

"What!?" Hazel exclaims. "How?"

"I didn't think it would catch anything on fire. I just wanted to see what it did. It was steel wool and a 9-volt battery."

I reel back and almost fall off the beam I'm sitting on.

"You okay?" Trace says.

"I'm up," I say and head to the start line.

Bree calls to me, "Let's see you burn up this course."

I glare at her, and she blows me a kiss.

"You know you're my favorite," she teases.

"All right, all right," Tully intervenes. "Save it for Valentine's Day."

I'm not nearly as fast as Bree in the suicides, but I am faster than Karmen and Hazel. The buffalo vault is easy, as is the wall climb up to the trampoline. I miss the bar and fall into the pit on my first try. On the second try, I get the bar, but my hands are a bit raw from practice, and I fall again. On the third time, I make the swing and make it to the barn. Now my hands are stinging. After I cross the beams and before I make my jump off the roof, I look down. Fifteen feet is a lot taller than any jump I've ever done, and a bad jump could end in a broken arm or collarbone. I imagine a dozen different poor outcomes.

From the mat below, Bree shoots me in the head with a dart and yells, "Jump! Like your life depends on it!"

I jump, but I make a big mistake. I hit the floor too hard, with not enough flexibility in my back and legs. Tully stops the clock, checks me out and announces that I will live.

"Carry on, from the trampoline," Tully says. He sets the timer back. I jump and grab the horizontal bar, and it tears at the skin of my palms, but I kick my knees back, and with two swings I am higher than the bar. Knees and feet are a very important part of Parkour. They help you build momentum, which is the only way you'll get anywhere. Friction is also important because it keeps you in place. Momentum plus friction lets us defy gravity.

I release the bar, grab the barn wall and walk up. Crossing the beams again, my hands burn, and my heart pounds. I count my heartbeats. Five heartbeats later I make the jump into a perfect safety roll. Trace, Hazel and Karmen shout and cheer. I'm more confident now as I vault over the hitching post, weave through the killer non-native crawdads, and clear the last wall. I'm at the scorpion-filled desert, a few leaps away from the end. A kong vault over the foam block and there it is. The camel.

I grab the camel around the neck and dash, zigzag across the cactus field (the part of the cactus played by everyone's socks) toward the barn. Bree points her foam dart gun at me and fires until she's emptied the gun, but still hasn't hit me, so she throws scorpions. I'm almost to the barn when one hits me in the leg. I throw the camel which flies right through the barn window.

Everyone shouts and claps, even Tully. Not Bree, who declares that I was killed by a scorpion before I could secure the camel.

"Don't worry about her," Trace says. "She doesn't give you the grade. Tully does."

Then he pulls me aside and says, "Over winter break, if you want to practice, me and some guys will be working out at Constitution Park. No Bree. These guys are cool and real athletes. I think you're ready for it."

"Yeah, okay," I say, though the idea of meeting new kids makes me feel sick, like another first day of school.

"Great! We meet at nine this Saturday," Trace says. "Bring it!"

Chapter 29

Urban Assault

Freddy, the bus driver, and I talk about Minecraft and Parkour while I'm riding home on Wednesdays. It makes the ride go by fast to talk about things I like. Freddy helps me keep count of the stops and calls out the landmarks if I miss one. He's a cool guy, and sometimes he allows me to pull the lever that opens and shuts the bus door.

Today is the last day of school before Winter Break, and I have something to show him. After I scan my bus pass, I pull out my report card.

"Freddy, I got one A and four Cs and only one D+!" I announce.

"Get outta here!" Freddy exclaims. "That's fantastic, son."

"I got Cs in History, Algebra, Latin, and Chemistry. The D+ was English. Guess where I got an A."

"Hmm," Freddy pretends he's thinking hard while he keeps his eyes on the road and uses his turn signal. "I'm going to guess it's that Parkour class. Am I right?"

"Yep! I got an A." I watch out the window feeling proud, not just because I did something right, but because I did something hard.

Mom tears up a little when she sees my report card. She says she wants to give me something special for my good grades. What I want is my mom and dad back together, but I'm not getting that. I already got one thing I wanted: a report card that didn't make me want to hide. But Mom says that doesn't count because it wasn't a gift. It was something I earned and worked hard for. I tell her I would like my own computer.

"If I get a good Christmas bonus, definitely."

"For real?"

"For real! And there's one more thing."

"You don't have to buy me anything else," I protest. I still feel guilty every day that all her stuff got burned up, too.

"Actually, it's about your dad. He has a job and a place to stay now. He would like you to spend a week with him over winter break. Would you like to do that?"

I haven't hugged my mom in a long time, but today, I hug her so hard she laughs and says I am choking her.

It's crispy cold on the roof that night, so I haul a quilt up with me. I lay on the roof and list all the good things that have happened lately. My grades are the best they've ever been. I got invited to practice with real athletes. I'll finally have a new computer. Best of all, I get to spend a week with my dad. I feel like I need to say thank you to the stars after all the time I've spent wishing on them. Mom calls it sending it out to the universe. Good manners required. So I say thank you to the universe for all the good things that have happened. Just in case it's listening.

Because, as everyone knows, sometimes a good thing can go terribly wrong.

On Saturday morning Mom drives me to Constitution Park to meet Trace and his friends. Trace and two other boys are on the bleachers by the ball field, jumping with both feet up the steps then diving onto the grass below.

"Hey!" Trace calls. "You made it!" The two boys jump off the bleachers and Trace introduces them.

"This is Caliente," he says, pointing to the one with red hair.

"And that's Razor." Razor has long blond hair pulled into a ponytail.

"Are those your real names?"

They all laugh. Trace says, "It's a Parkour thing. Once you find your style, you get a name. Usually, your friends come up with it. He's called Caliente because one day, he was literally on fire when he leaped over a fire pit and caught his pants. Razor is crazy good at crossing anything narrow like he could walk on the edge of a razor wire and not even twitch."

Caliente says, "And Without a Trace here can disappear from sight, just poof and he's gone."

"Trace is your Parkour name?" I ask, amused.

"Yep. My real name is Leonard. Did you know that Bree stands for Breeze? Because she's so fast all you feel is the breeze go by."

"You got a name yet?" Razor asks. I shake my head.

"My Minecraft name is BackgroundNoise."

Trace looks at me thoughtfully. "I think that's perfect for you! You're the quiet guy in the background, but when you get going, you bring da' noise!"

"All right then, Noise, get warmed up and let's see what you can do. We're practicing the urban assault course today," Caliente says.

We do squats, pull-ups, push-ups, and burpees. We run a 200-meter sprint and monkey style quadrupedal. Then we run the 200-meter backward. We take a water break while Caliente, who is the oldest of us at fifteen years old, draws the urban assault course in the dirt with a stick.

Urban assault is what they call going from an open space area, like Constitution Park, across a neighborhood of small houses and into downtown Phoenix, all the way to the baseball stadium. That's how Caliente explains it, but it's a lot more complicated than it sounds.

"Stand right here and tell me what you see." Caliente points me to the far side of the golf course.

I look across the park and see chain link fences separating the ball fields, the cement walls of the skateboard bowls and jumps, a lagoon with a building that houses the snack bar, bicycle rentals and paddle boats tied to a wooden dock. That's as far as I can see, then fences block the view of the houses beyond the park.

"Golf course is off limits. Plus, it's boring. We go straight to the center of the action until we get to the neighborhood. Take in what you can see, plan your approach, commit to the move, all in about three seconds," Caliente says. "Everyone ready?"

He counts down 3-2-1 then shouts "Go!" and just like that, Trace is in the lead. He's the first one across the ball fields, vaulting over three low fences. Caliente is next followed by Razor, then me. The skate park comes up, and the wall that surrounds the bowls dips low and slopes up as if a giant were tipping his cereal bowl. We run along the wall to its highest point then leap off onto the grass.

Just before that, when I'm up high, I see it.

The world isn't grass, trees, houses, and cars. The world is a grid made of lines, platforms, fences, and blocks. It's a Minecraft course, with geometric shapes, lanes, lines, and tunnels. The small details disappear, and I only see what I need to see: a path in every direction. My head fills with a sound like cicadas in the trees, a buzzing that drowns out bad thoughts. Like tracing a path through the stars with my finger. The only thing I want to do is keep moving along the top of the maze.

The way through is easy to see when you're up high. I knew that, but now I understand it.

For once in my life, I'm not feeling my way through the dark and bumping into things I can't move out of the way. I'm not being dragged from one place to another trying to remember what I am supposed to be doing. I'm not stuck with a million choices.

"Don't stop," Caliente says, dropping back to coach me through the paddle boats. "You're doing great!"

We move in a line, one at a time, over the bars, walls, benches, the metal bike racks and onto the wooden boat dock. Trace and Razor go right across the paddle boats that are tied up in a neat row, like floating lily pads. Their feet skim the things they are flying over, but it's like they get energy from them. People step back, watch in amazement and clap when we go by. We're there and gone so fast, there isn't even time to say hello.

When we get past the boat dock, I collapse on the strip of grass that borders the park and the houses behind it. Trace, Razor, and Caliente stop with me, breathing heavy and walking in circles, high-fiving each other.

"You are the Noise!" Caliente says, fist bumping. "First outdoor course?"

"Sort of," I say. "I do stuff at my apartment complex, off the roof and the playground."

Caliente points to the block wall fence across the grass.

"Public space is one thing, but neighborhoods are another. Keep a sharp eye on cars and people. We don't want anyone getting hurt or getting mad. Stick to the yards and alleys and don't jump down into anyone's yard. We basically travel from fence to fence and the occasional shed or rooftop. We can make it almost all the way to the stadium without ever touching the ground."

Trace grins at me.

"What?"

"You've got it," he says.

"Got what?"

"The sight. You can see it, can't you?"

I look back at the park and then ahead at the low rooftops peeking above the fences.

"I think so."

Fist bumps all around and we are off again. Without ever touching the ground.

CHAPTER 30

TACOS AND LIES

Dad is late.

I sit outside on my suitcase holding my backpack, which contains my new laptop, and grow more and more worried as the minutes tick by. What if he doesn't come? What if he never comes? What if what if what if what if?

Mom sticks her head out the front door a couple times to check on me. She calls him to make sure he is still coming. He doesn't answer. I feel sick to my stomach, and my head feels woozy. When I finally hear the diesel engine grind around the corner, I scramble to my feet.

"Whoa, that's a lot of stuff for a few days," he says as I place my bag in the truck. I scoot across the seat to hug him, but he pulls back.

"Watch the cigarette," he says and pats me on the shoulder instead.

Dad dangles his left arm out the open window every few minutes to flick off the ashes. He doesn't look at me. He messes with the radio and pounds a fist on the dash when it won't come on. When he speaks, it's like he's only just realized I am here.

"Hey! So, how's school?"

"Good." I start to tell him how we flew like ninjas across Constitution Park all the way to the ball field. Trace invited me next Saturday for the next course, beginning at the park lake, through the campus of Arizona State University. But Dad's cell phone rings and he answers it. He talks to someone else like I'm not here. A wall slams down on my head, and all the things I want to tell him are trapped on the other side.

When we get to his house, I'm surprised to see other people are living there. Two men sit on a sofa watching television and eating hamburgers out of Dave's Burger Joint bags. Man #1 doesn't look up when we walk in. Man Number Two nods at us as we walk past into a hallway.

Dad points to the end of the hallway and says, "My room is down there."

"Your room?"

"Yeah, a few other guys live here, too," he says. "Hey, it's better than a parking lot, right?"

Dad's room has a mattress on the floor and a dresser and a couple of cardboard boxes full of clothes.

"This place has a huge backyard. Wanna see it?"

We go to the kitchen, where Man Number Three, is making a sandwich.

"This your boy?"

"Yeah, this is Jeremy. He's going to stay with me for a few days."

"You want a baloney sandwich?" Man Number Three asks.

"No, thanks. I'm not supposed to have processed meat or gluten."

He chuckles and says, "Okay, good luck with that around here."

Dad says, "You can have whatever you want, Jeremy. There's root beer in the fridge."

Dad grabs a bag of spicy corn chips from the counter, and I take a can of root beer from the fridge, which is packed with sodas and not much else. Outside, there are lawn chairs, a long green hose snaking across the shaggy grassy yard, and super tall trees and oleanders that reach up to the power lines. There's also an old woodshed with a metal roof and a cement patio. Dad and I sit on the lawn chairs. He digs into his shirt pocket and pulls out a package of cigarettes.

"I thought you quit."

"Don't worry about it," he says. He opens the chips and offers me the bag. "So, what do you want to do today?"

"This is okay." I'm checking out the fences and the house to see what I can get on top of. "Who are those people?"

"Just guys. We all work at the same place. You wanna go see a movie?"

I want to tell my dad what I did yesterday with Trace and the team. That I got one A, three Cs, and one D+. I want him to see my new laptop. I want to tell him about the summer camp contest, show him how I can practically fly from one side of the yard to the other, never touching the grass. But I can't. It feels wrong. It always feels wrong to tell him things that I am excited about when he is in the dumps. Like he is still sitting at a table in Dave's Burger Joint, not watching, while I'm in a tube above him, wondering when he'll look up. Or he's sitting on that stupid rock in the neighbor's yard while our house burns and he never once looks over at Mom and me. That's what I see when I look at him putting out his cigarette on the concrete patio, even though there is an ashtray a few feet away. He looks like someone that bad things have happened to and hearing about good things that are happening to someone else will only make him sadder.

My dad is here, but he isn't here. That's the way it is. That's the way it's always been. I'm like one of the things he carries in his pockets. A bottle cap he likes to take out and look at sometimes. He doesn't want to toss it out because it belongs there, but it's in the way of other stuff he wants to have. I'm a thing in the collection of things that didn't burn up in the fire. He has his truck. A room. Some clothes. Cigarettes and a lighter. A home that is not a parking lot. A son. In no particular order of importance.

"So, let's head to the mall. Catch a movie. Get some tacos," he says. I follow him back into the house. None of the men say anything or even look up. When we leave, Dad locks the bedroom door behind him.

We go see a superhero movie. I notice that a lot of the tricks the superheroes do are Parkour. I want to tell Dad what the moves are called, but I don't. During the movie, he gets up three times to smoke outside. The third time, he doesn't come back before the movie ends. I wait in my seat until everyone has left the theater and the credits run, and lights come up, not sure if I should stay where I am so he can find me, or if I should go look for him. I walk out into the theater lobby and push through the people going the other way to the exit.

When the crowd filters through for the next showing and the lobby is almost empty, he's still not here. I wait on a bench in front of a movie poster of a huge zombie guy and feel like I am going to throw up spicy corn chips, root beer and popcorn with too much butter flavoring. I can't sit here anymore. My dad is nowhere in sight.

The food court is packed with kids and their parents. I walk around the food court three times, checking every restaurant, but I don't find him. I'm going to throw up, and I don't know where the bathroom is, so I make my way to the mall exit and go outside and sit on a bench. It's nighttime, and the cool air makes me feel better. I remember he said something about tacos, so I head back inside to the food court, and there he is, sitting at the tables at Taco Shack. He pushes a tray of tacos at me.

"Where'd you go?" I ask. "I looked all over for you."

"I told you to meet me here when the movie was over."

I pick up a taco and then put it down again. It's still hot in the wrapper.

"Sorry," I say. Even though I know, he is lying.

CHAPTER 31

SLAM. CLICK. GOODBYE.

Next to my dad on the mattress, I can't sleep. It's cold in here, and the one blanket on the bed is mostly underneath my dad, who is snoring. Both of us are sleeping in our clothes. I go into the kitchen to look for something to eat. There's leftover pizza in the fridge, a half-empty jar of mustard, a partial loaf of bread and a package of baloney. No vegetables. No plate of food ready to eat with plastic wrap. A bag of pretzels is open on the counter, so I eat a few, but they are dry and lumpy going down. I get a drink of water from the sink with my hand because I can't find a clean glass.

I put on my sweatshirt and go outside. There's a courtyard and a wall in the front, and I climb up on it and step up to the roof. Little houses, many of them outlined with holiday lights are all around us. It's a lot like the neighborhood I raced through last Saturday with Trace, Caliente, and Razor. I could easily get from this roof to the next and the next if I wanted to. If I only wanted to. I'm too tired, hungry, confused, and cold. Right now, I want my dad to be wondering where I am. But he doesn't wonder. He doesn't come looking. I don't want to be in his room, so I lay down on the roof and close my eyes.

When I wake up, it's dark, but the sun is just starting to

lighten the clouds. I climb down from the roof and go back into Dad's room. He's still sleeping. No one is awake in the house. I pick up my backpack to get my laptop, hoping this house has wifi. I immediately notice that my pack is open and my computer is gone. That's it. I'm done.

"Dad, wake up, Dad!" I holler at him. He doesn't even move. I shake his shoulder. "Dad, please! My laptop is gone, please wake up!"

He moves a little and pushes my arm away. "Stop," he says without opening his eyes.

"What's wrong?" It's Man Number Three standing in the doorway. "You okay, son?"

"No! My laptop is gone, and my dad won't wake up."

"Okay, calm down."

He walks into the room and nudges my dad with his foot.

"Hey, wake up, your kid needs you. Hey. Keith."

When he hears Number Three say his name, Dad opens his eyes and squints up at us. I fall on my knees next to the mattress.

"My laptop is gone! Mom just bought it for me. Please get up."

"You lock your room last night?" Asks Number Three.

"Huh? Yeah, of course."

"Keith, you been drinking?"

Dad doesn't answer. "Get out of my room," he says.

Man Number Three shakes his head.

"Sorry, son," he says. "I think we better call your mom."

He wakes up all the men in the house, and they all come out of their rooms and sit in the living room, not really awake. My dad gets up and heads for the kitchen.

"Give us a minute, please, Keith," Man Number Three says. My dad glares at him and puts the pack of cigarettes back in his pocket, then sits down. He doesn't even look at me.

Man Number Three says, "We have rules in this home, and we take them seriously. Jeremy's laptop has gone missing, and I'd like to have it returned to him pronto, or everyone here will be on probation until it is found."

I'm confused. Why is he in charge? I watch my dad who isn't saying anything and isn't looking at me; it's like I'm not even here. He should be searching the house for my laptop, but he's just sitting there. Then the doorbell rings. I can't help it. When I see Mom, I start to cry.

"I'm so sorry, Jeremy," she says. I let her hug me. "What happened?"

"We came home from the movies and went to bed. I woke up, and my laptop was gone. I couldn't get Dad to wake up." I leave out the part about going outside onto the roof and falling asleep. I'm braced for a scene. For the yelling that ties my stomach in knots and makes my head pound. But it doesn't happen. All the men, including my dad, are quiet. Mom picks up my backpack and my suitcase.

"Let's go, Jeremy," Mom says. She doesn't say a word to my dad.

"I have five days left!" I protest. I don't want to leave. I just want her to fix it.

"Jeremy, I'm sorry, but he's just not ready yet."

Dad doesn't look up or anything. He just sits there, his face in his hands, like the night of the fire. Like things aren't really falling to ashes around us if you don't look at them. But I'm not ready to give up on him yet. I walk over to him and put my arms around his shoulders and hug him. He puts his arms around me and hugs me back.

"See you later, kiddo," he says. Then he stands up and walks down the hall to his room.

"Maybe try again in a few weeks," Number Three says to my mom. "I'll let you know if we find the laptop. I'm really sorry, son."

Mom tries to talk to me on the ride home. She tries to feed me when we get there. But there is no comforting me. Into my room, up onto the bunk, back into the box where I can shut it all away.

Slam. Click. Goodbye.

CHAPTER 32

BREAK FALL

For the next few days, all I want to do is sleep. When Mom leaves for work, I don't even wake up or eat the breakfast she left in the fridge. There is nothing to do in the apartment except watch television, so that's pretty much all I do besides sleep. A couple times I go down to the playground, but there are other kids there, and I don't feel like being around them. Mom leaves me some cash in case I want to walk down the street for Hawaiian ice or go to Dave's. She's relaxed on the diet because I haven't eaten hardly anything for days. I go nowhere. I stop taking my meds.

My brain is tired, bored and sad. But it isn't quiet. It reviews the facts over and over.

My dad hasn't called, not even to say sorry. The laptop that was mine for forty-eight hours has not been returned. I once had a rubber band ball made of three thousand rubber bands in ten different colors. I once had a dog for three months before it ran away. We went to Disneyland for my fifth birthday. Just Mom and me because she and Dad had a fight the night before and he went somewhere else. In my brain, there are good things, but they are wrapped up in bad things.

It's hard to see them like they are the stars furthest away and only show up occasionally. It makes me tired.

On Saturday morning, Mom knocks on my door and won't go away until I answer her.

"What?"

"Get some clothes on, we need to leave soon."

"Where?"

"Just come on."

"Fine."

I know what she is doing. She doesn't like me sitting around the house. She's taking me to Parkour practice whether I want to go or not. I can tell, after five days not taking the meds, I move differently. I'm not as sharp. I feel a lot less sure of what I'm doing. I know it's going to be bad. I'll freeze up and make a wrong move and injure myself. Before, I knew when my feet needed to leave the ground. I knew when to lean back and trust the momentum to take me over the wall. I knew that when I threw everything I had at the wall, I would be up and over in two giant steps.

She puts my blue pill, and a new white one, on the table next to breakfast.

"The white one is for anxiety," she says, sitting down. "By the way, Trace called again."

I pick the eggs with my fork. There are green onions and tomatoes. Like a punishment.

"Jeremy, there are things you can change in your life, and there are things you can't control. Your dad and what he does is not in your control. It never will be. I can't control it either."

I picked up my fork to eat the eggs that I've picked clean of green onions and tomatoes. Maybe if I eat, she'll stop talking about it.

"But there are things you can change. The meds help you make those changes. I've seen big changes in you since you started Parkour. You have friends calling. You do homework on time. You talk about things you love. At least you did. Before the thing with your dad."

"Okay. Stop," I say. She gets up and walks into the kitchen. "Finish your eggs and take the meds, Jeremy. We are leaving in five minutes."

Trace, Razor, and Caliente are doing standing front flips in the grass.

"Noise, you made it!" Trace says with a fist bump. "Watch this."

It happens so fast I can't even see how they do it. One second they are standing there, the next their bodies curl up into blurry balls that unfold into bodies again and land on their feet. Almost in sync with each other.

"You were still late, Trace, but better!" Caliente says. He looks at me. "You ready to try it?"

"I don't know."

"Yeah, you're doing it," Razor says. "We'll help you. But first, go run a few laps and warm up. You look like you haven't moved in a week."

He's right. My hair is stringy. I haven't showered for a couple days. I stink.

I run three laps around the field, then Razor and Caliente talk me through the hardest move I've tried so far: the standing front flip.

For a move that is over in under two seconds, every step is critical and must be done precisely, or you'll end up flat on your back, your face, or worse, your head. I practice taking a few running steps forward, swing my arms up to the sky, while I jump, pushing my body up as high as I can. I do this dozen of times until I get the right height.

In the next step, we modify the jump. Instead of straight legs, I pull my knees up tight to my chest. I concentrate on keeping my knees apart, or I could smack my chin. I also practice dive rolls, to make sure I can flip my body over my head without freaking out. I already know how to do that, because it's required in the Old West course.

Now for the hard part: putting everything together. Jump and simultaneously swing arms up. At the precise moment before hitting the peak of the jump, swing the arms down. To rotate forward in the air, you must give up something that is very scary to give up. You tuck your head into your chest, which pulls your body into a rotation but eliminates your ability to see where you are going to land. That's the hardest part for me. I always want to know where I am going to land. Now I must rely on doing everything perfectly and then go blind.

"This is the most important thing you have to do that is all in your head, not your body," says Caliente. "You have to commit. Once you start the rotation, you cannot stop, or you'll be like a plane falling out of the sky. It's not pretty. No hesitation. Get your head fully into the move. If you don't think you can do that, abort into a break fall."

A break fall is how you land on your back without hurting yourself. It's a hard jolt that can knock the breath right out of you or give you a concussion.

"Jump, tuck, rotate, land," Caliente says. "Got that? Repeat it in your mind."

I punch into my jump from the ground, eyes to the sky, tuck in my shoulders while thrusting up my knees, then tip my head forward. I land flat on my back with a thunk!

Caliente says, "You didn't commit."

I try it again. Thunk. And again. I nail the spin but don't get enough height, so I land on my tailbone instead of my back. Thunk. Thunk. Thunk.

I'm wondering if I know how to commit when Trace says, "Try closing your eyes. Think about the one thing you wish for the most."

I'm not sure this will help. Choosing one thing is never easy for me. I stand for a minute before I even move and then when I move my arms into the swing, wishing goes something like this.

Jump. I wish for friends.

Tuck. I wish I was smart.

Rotate. I wish I was normal.

Land. I wish my dad was here.

When I open my eyes, the guys looked stunned. Then they break into a loud cheer.

"Dude! That was sick!" Trace yells. High-fives all around. I'm smiling and can't even talk. One wish out of four? Not bad, given my history.

CHAPTER 33

MINDFULNESS

"Mindfulness," booms Tully's voice over the mic when I am rushing in, late, on the first day back from holiday break. I couldn't find my shoes. I forgot my lunch. Mom made me responsible for remembering to take the blue and white pills, and I forgot, and we had to turn around.

"Mind/Ful/Ness." He writes it out like just that on the board. "What is it? Yes, Stanley."

"When your brain, which is also your mind, is full of something," Stanley answers.

"Yes. Thank you, Stanley. Other thoughts? Students of Latin?"

Hazel, who has a question answering competition going on with Bree, raises her hand.

"Mindful in Latin is memor, which means remembering, grateful, or thoughtful."

"It does, indeed. Can anyone take it one step further?"

Bree, who has let everyone know many times that she is getting an A in Latin, speaks.

"It's also about being aware of something. Like, paying attention." She shoots a look of satisfaction at Hazel.

"All correct answers. Thank you. Mindfulness, in a word, is awareness. To be mindful is to be very aware of what your brain is doing, or to paraphrase Stanley, what fills your mind. Can you name one thing you are all doing right this very second that you are not usually aware of doing?"

"Sleeping," whispers Trace. Ben, David and I stifle laughter.

"Breathing," answers Bree, who gives us all the glare of death.

"Yes, Bree. Let's think about breathing. I would like everyone to fold your hands on the table in front of you, close your eyes, and be mindful of the breath you are taking in and the breath you are blowing out. Keep going until I tell you to stop."

Dr. Nugent demonstrates in front of the room. Her hands are still in front of her, and her eyes are closed.

Tully repeats, "Breath in, breath out."

The room fills with sounds of people drawing deep breaths and blowing them out. Tully keeps talking.

"Focus, for many of us in this room, is a daily struggle. A minute to minute struggle. When you detect your attention is wandering from what you are supposed to be doing, take one full minute to stop and be mindful of your breath in and your breath out. Anytime you feel stressed, bored, angry, worried, or even sleepy, try mindfulness to bring you back on track."

It's the longest minute ever when Tully finally says, "Open

your eyes. That was one full minute."

Some days, I think Tully is just weird. That's what I am mindful of when he taps me on the shoulder as we are leaving for the first period and asks me to come to his office.

Dr. Nugent is there, too. Tully slides a copy of my report card to Dr. Nugent, who looks it over.

"Relax, Jeremy, you aren't in trouble."

My first semester grades were better than I thought they would be, but I still got a D+ in Language, and my C slipped to a D in Chemistry. That's what they want to talk about. My failures.

"Great final project score! It saved you from an F in Chemistry," Tully notes, "I can see that lab reports and homework assignments are hard for you."

Right now, I am mindful of feeling stupid. Also, I am sitting on a yoga ball. It's hard not to bounce up and down on it while my feet work on staying in one place. This is supposed to help the kids who can't sit still, like Trace. He says it's like scratching a mosquito bite that never goes away. Sitting still used to be hard for me, too, but if I am doing something interesting, I can sit all day and do it. Like Minecraft. But if I'm not sure what to do I fidget with stuff. Homework, for example. I try hard to get all the writing assignments done, not only for Chemistry but Language, History, and Latin. I sit for hours sometimes, and my brain goes somewhere else entirely.

It looks like I'm zoning out, but it's the opposite. I wish I could just let the teachers see inside my head where everything is coming together. I imagine them opening my brain and picking around in it with chopsticks, moving the gray matter around, trying to find something that makes sense. But it's a mess in there. It's layers and layers of stuff that connects in different ways, like the 3D model of a Krypton atom I built for my final Chemistry project out of marshmallows and toothpicks.

"What did you think about our talk this morning?" Dr. Nugent asks.

I shrug.

"What happened when you tried the mindfulness exercise?"

"Nothing, really."

Dr. Nugent slides something across the table to me. It's a small MP3 player and a set of earbuds.

"Use this while you try something for me," she says. "Think about your breathing. Take a breath in and count one hydrogen molecule, two hydrogen molecules, then exhale."

I put the earbuds in and turn on the music. I hear an acoustic guitar and a light, steady drumbeat. I leave the office with the MP3 player in my pocket. I'm allowed to use it during study time and quiet time in the classroom. I decide against using a yoga ball, mostly because it's so big. Everyone will see.

But when I get to class, I see Trace and two other kids sitting on yoga balls. No one is looking at them weird except me. I take a seat next to Trace, and Mr. Anderson points me to the problem set for the day.

Trace looks content, slowly rocking back and forth on the ball. I listen to the music thrumming in my brain. Before I know it, I'm asleep with my head on the table.

CHAPTER 34

DreAdED_FrEakShow

Mr. Anderson shakes me awake. I'm drooling on the table. I'm embarrassed, but no one else seems to notice or care. Everyone is part of the chaos that is math class. Yoga balls, pipe cleaners, bags of candy, fidget cubes, puzzles, chewable pencil toppers, MP3 players like mine. Not one of us is just sitting here doing math. Every one of us is doing math while doing something else. Mr. Anderson tells me to try music that is a little more energetic and finds a playlist that has more drums and electric guitar.

I restart the problem set. When I leave math class, I'm finished and pleased with myself.

That feeling goes away fast when I see my locker. It's been papered with drawings. Three of them. In the first is a house and a person in a window looking out. In the next drawing, the person holds up a torch to the curtain. In the last picture, the house is only a tiny puff of smoke coming up from the ground. Next to it is a small, unhappy person with empty circles for eyes.

Someone put a lot of work into this.

Trace and Hazel look at my locker with their heads tilted, like dogs trying to figure out what a sound is. Hazel reaches over and pulls off one of the pictures. On the flip side of the drawing, it says, "I know what you did."

"Bree," Hazel says angrily. "She's got to be stopped."

"What does it mean?" Trace says. "Did your house burn down or something?"

I rip the papers off the locker door and crumple them up. Sometimes having smart friends is a problem. They figure stuff out about you that you don't want them to know.

"It's nothing." Hazel and Trace help me strip all the tape and paper off my locker door. I open the door cautiously, expecting something to tumble out. But nothing does. Instead, everything in my locker is coated with something white and powdery.

"It's like a smoke bomb went off in there." Hazel fans the air. Trace claps his hand on my shoulder.

"Dude, don't worry about it. We'll help you clean it up."

We determine that the white stuff is shaving cream. It's dried into a sticky powder. I take everything out of my locker and Hazel brings wet paper towels from the bathroom to wipe off my books and binders. But we have little time. The class bell rings, and we rush to cram everything back in.

"Go ahead without me. I'll finish cleaning it up and be late.

While I'm angrily scrubbing the powdery stuff out of my locker, I put in the earbuds and turn on the music, and try not think about all the good things that turned bad. The new laptop was mine for two days before it disappeared. Months with no word from my dad. Then my dad, showing up which I thought was a good thing but then, it wasn't.

This stuff smells like soap. I think it is dry shampoo. My mom made me try that once when I was going through a phase where I didn't like to get my head wet.

Dr. Nugent comes around the corner and sees me at my locker.

"Hey, Jeremy, what's going on? I heard you weren't in class." She peers into my locker. I hurriedly gather up the paper towel pile from the floor and take it to the trashcan.

"Something spilled in my locker." I feel like I am four years old again and Miss Emily is trying to save me from Miss Pat's bruising fingers. It's the expression on her face. I can't even look her in the eyes.

"I'll walk you to class," she says. I shut my locker door and step back. There are still shreds of tape all over it. We walk down the hall to the secret Minecraft room, and Dr. Nugent knocks two times then pauses and knocks three times fast. The door opens, and Turnbull's smile emerges out of the dark room.

"Hello, Jeremy!" He says enthusiastically. "And, hello Dr. Nugent!"

"Sorry, I kept him a few minutes late. Have a great day, Jeremy!" She walks away.

Trace glances up at me, a green glow on his face, looking relieved. I take an empty station next to him and sign on to my *BackgroundNoise* account.

"Trace, please show Jeremy our new project for this week," Turnbull asks. Trace leans over and whispers.

"What happened?"

"Nothing," I whisper back. "She just walked me to class. I think she suspects something though."

I sneak a glance across the room at Bree, who is staring right at us. Just then a chat pops up on my screen. It's a screen name I don't recognize: DreAdED_FrEakShow.

Give me food, and I will live. Give me water, and I will die. What am I?

"It's her," Trace says. "Do you know the answer?"

"I'm thinking."

"We're going to need some professional help," Trace says. He types a message to me, BenLordValor and DavidMonkee.

"DreAdED_FrEakShow has launched a missile at BackgroundNoise. Activate Trojan Dragon to target: DreAdED_FrEakShow"

BenLordValor replies, "Activating Trojan Dragon".

DavidMonkee replies, "Trojan Dragon loaded. Initiating in five seconds".

I can't explain how the thought comes to me, it just did. Bree can't be the one who drew the pictures taped to my locker.

No way is she that good at art without bragging about herself all the time. She has terrible handwriting. Whoever drew these was slow and careful with the details. She had to enlist the help of someone who was good at art. Someone who would follow her blindly and maybe not even suspect that she was using them to hurt someone. Someone who isn't in it for revenge or to win the summer camp contest. Someone who would do it for Bree and Bree alone. Innocent and unsuspecting. Only one person I know fits that description.

I message Trace, Ben, and David: Abort Trojan Dragon! It's not Bree!

I'm too late. We've unleashed a fierce, fire-breathing demon that suddenly takes over the screen of its unsuspecting owner and roars a throatful of fire. Bree doesn't flinch. But Jeremy the Younger looks up from the screen. His eyes are big. He shoves back his chair, stands up and flaps his hands like they are on fire and he is trying to put them out. Bree jumps out of her seat and puts her hands on his shoulders.

"Calm down, calm down," she says to him, "Look at me." Then she sees his screen. Her eyes shift to me. I mouth the answer to the riddle.

Fire.

Turnbull springs into action. He guides Jeremy the Younger, who is now trying to get out of the room, back into his seat. Bree knows the drill with her brother. She hands him a bottle of water from her bag which he grabs and holds close to his chest.

Trace messages, "How did you know it was J the Y and not Bree?"

I reply, "Lucky guess."

CHAPTER 35

ZIPLINE

"Unbelievable," Hazel says when we see her in Room 3.14. "She's awful. Using her own brother for her dirty deeds."

We are moving around the blocks and walls to make a new course that we designed in the Minecraft room using a mod that Trace found. Bree is across the room, climbing a rope to a new, higher platform that was installed while we were away at winter break. It's called the tree house. After you climb the rope, there are three ways to exit the tree house. One is a set of rings that cross the foam pit. Another is a rope bridge. The third is a zipline that cruises across the room and lands onto a thick, squishy foam mattress. We used algebra, geometry, trigonometry, physics, and engineering to design it. The zipline was the hardest part. It has to be the right height off the ground so that our feet wouldn't drag. The length of the cable has to provide for no more than five percent sag, considering the maximum weight of the trolley and the rider. If the angle is too steep, the rider will travel too fast and could get hurt.

It's the most intense course we've had all year, and we learn new moves to complete it. Every run we do now is timed. Tully says it adds a new layer of complication that our brains must calculate while we are in motion.

"I'm not sure I understand," Trace says, tugging on the mattress that is our landing pad. "Why is she using her brother to intimidate us?

I shake my head. I seriously have no idea.

"It's just wrong," Hazels says. "The poor kid didn't expect it, and he doesn't like surprises."

I don't like surprises, either. That makes sense to me. Even good ones, like when Mom said she was going to buy me a new laptop. I was happy while conjuring a jillion ways I could mess it up. And then. So, yeah, I guess I do understand why Jeremy the Younger freaked out.

We finish setting up the course, and Tully gets ready to demonstrate.

At the timer, Bree yells, "Go!"

Tully sprints. First, he scales a wall that connects the rope bridge to the tree house and dashes across the bridge. Then he swings hand to hand through the rings to the alley, a network of connected walls with bars. The idea is you never touch the ground. He precision jumps across a six-foot span, then wall to wall then back to the tree house platform to his zipline finale. Joey is on the platform with the harness and helps Tully slip it on. Tully clicks his carabiner onto the trolley and off he goes.

He hits feet first into the squishy mattress and leaps off. Karmen is there as a spotter, in case of emergency.

Tully calls it the "ecosystem of teamwork." Without every single person doing their part, the whole course is a colossal failure, and someone will get injured. Just like in the living, real ecosystems we are studying in Biology. In Parkour, everyone has a job to do. Because this is the most difficult course we have done, only one person can be on the course at a time while the rest of us are placed where we can help in case the runner gets in trouble. It's kind of like a relay race. Bree gets ready to run, I take Karmen's place as landing pad spotter, Karmen moves to the alley, Trace takes the rope bridge, Hazel is on the overlook at the six-foot span, and Joey is on the timer. Tully takes the tree house to help each of us with the harness. The landing pad spotter is the last to go, the timer watcher is first.

When it's my turn, Bree is on the timer. I have no trouble with the course, though the rope bridge throws me off a little until I remember that the faster you go across it, the easier it is. When I get to the tree house platform, Tully helps me into the harness.

Then I make a rookie mistake. I linger. Just long enough to think about what I'm about to do. I should be zipping down already. But I don't leap off the platform. I'm scared.

I haven't been this scared before in Parkour. Not when I first went over a wall or a fence. Not even when I learned a standing front flip. But faced with an aircraft cable, a steel pulley, a cloth harness and a bunch of clips and bolts, a whole lot more can go wrong than just falling. The braking system could fail. The pulley could get caught up. The carabiner could snap off. My head swims with possibilities of unlikely but catastrophic failure.

"You've got this," Tully says behind me. "It's effortless flying. Breathe and let go. Trust your team. Trust yourself."

Tully's voice is steady. Breathe in, breathe out, breathe in, breathe out. Effortless flying. I think about the origami cranes Dr. Nugent made when she was still Miss Emily. She said there was a legend that if you made one thousand cranes, your wish would come true. Then she slipped me a crane, a special one whose wings moved up and down when you tugged on the tail.

"Why one thousand?" I asked.

"Because it's hard. It takes persistence and dedication and long hours of tedious work. But the rewards are splendid. What would you wish for?"

It's one of those things that enter my head when it's quiet when I can hear thoughts one at a time instead of piled on top of each other. What would I wish for?

I breathe in. I breathe out. I step off the platform, and I'm airborne. My brain wants to calculate my acceleration rate and speed. In less than five seconds, my decline slows, and I cruise easily to a halt at the landing pad.

Everyone cheers for me. Tully punches the air with his fists.

Except for Bree, the timer in hand steps onto the scene and ruins everything.

"You took one minute longer than anyone to complete the course. Even Hazelnut beat you."

Inside an alarm sounds. My heart races. I look Bree right in the face. She's taller than me. She's smiling with not a drop of worry, while sweat and heat pour out of my skin. I clench my fists and words fly out of me.

"I don't care what my time was. I don't even care if I win the contest. I don't like you, and I don't like how you treat people. I don't like how you treat your brother. Stop messing with me and stop messing with my friends."

I grab my pack and walk out of Room 3.14. I'm trembling, my heart is racing, and my head pounds. I pass my locker. I pass Dr. Nugent's office. I ignore Tully calling my name. I throw open the front doors of the school, and as my feet hit the sidewalk, I sprint down the sidewalk away from the school. I don't know where I'm going until I see Bus Number Twoo turn the corner and head for my bus stop. I wave to Freddy, and he stops and opens the door. I toss my pack onto a seat.

"Hello there! This isn't Wednesday. Is everything okay?"

"How long does it take to get to my bus stop?"

"Twenty minutes or so. You coming on?"

"Nope. I'll see you there."

CHAPTER 36

HESITATION

I sprint ahead of the bus as it lurches forward. Next up is the Arizona Science Center. It covers the entire city block, and the main building is surrounded by cement walls of different heights. I need to go from one side of the science center to the other. I could go around it, but the sidewalk is jammed with school kids lined up for a field trip. Plus, going around is the opposite of Parkour.

Go through, not around. I look for the shortest, simplest way to cross the massive science center. I run along the top of the wall that surrounds the building, passing up school kids in line, dive roll to the ground and clear the steps down to the next level in one jump. I vault over planters of shrubs and even a man sleeping on a bench. At the top of the steps leading down to the street level, I slide down the handrail, past a dozen or so people making their way up.

One stop down. Six to go.

Downtown Phoenix is full of trash cans and benches and other obstacles like people waiting for trains. I'm now at the light rail station. Just to the left of me is the pedestrian bridge that takes people safely across six lanes of traffic. I'm at the busiest intersection in downtown. We practiced stairs, going up and down, at Constitution Park. These stairs have landings where the steps change direction. The way up is straight up. Skip the stairs completely. Wall walk up the first flight. From there, jump up wall to wall until you're at the top. At the bridge, I sprint across. It takes me only three jumps down to the ground when I reach the stairs on the other side.

Next, I'm at the open-air market filled with benches, garden planters, vendors underneath pop-up tents, carts, and umbrellas. When I scan the plaza, I see my way. The plaza has five large planters, about four feet high. I run and hurdle those. Cafe tables are scattered around, blocking the path to the other side. Most of the tables are empty, so I go right over them to the barricades that block the market from the street. Lazy vault over those.

I take a rest but not for long. Four stops to go. I see the bus pulling away from stop Number Three, and I know that in another block, Bus Number Twoo will make its turn to stop Number Four. I need to get there, or I'll get too far behind. The bus goes around the parking garage, but I need to go through it. There is no other way to get to the stop Number Four.

Caliente loves parking garages. They are a fast way across a city block, all stairs, and walls, and easy kong vaults. I cross the entrance swinging monkey style from pipe to pipe. Suspended horizontally from the low ceiling, this takes me swiftly over parked cars, like the rings over our foam pit. I vault a few wall barriers and sprint across the second level of the garage where a car almost runs me down. I'm just about to vault over the second level wall and down to the grass on the other side, but a driver lays on his horn and I'm distracted, so I divert to the stairwell, pull myself up and over the last two stair landings.

I'm on the top level, three stories up. It's busy with cars coming and going. I look over the edge of the wall, and I see grass, huge trees, and beyond that, the edge of Constitution Park. There's no way out except straight down or the way I came in. But that will take too long.

Bus Number Twoo turns the corner. I can't make this jump. I could break my collarbone, a leg, or an arm. My heart is thumping too fast to count. I shouldn't have come up to the top.

I pace beside the wall, angry with myself. I push my palms against my temples, feel my pulse and focus on my breathing. Slow my heartbeats. Breathe in. Breathe out. Trust your team. Trust yourself. You've got this. There are trees and grass that make for a soft landing. A dive roll to slow the momentum, so I don't break a bone. I know the way in my head.

But it's a long way down, and I hesitate. Bus Number Twoo pulls away.

CHAPTER 37

THE WHY

Time has run out. I must do this. In my head, I can see myself doing it, but I also see myself doing it wrong. I tell myself *if I make this jump my dad will come home. If I make this jump, everything will be okay.* I don't even care if it's a lie. I climb up on the wall and try to calm myself the way Caliente taught me.

What would I wish for?

I know my dad did some stupid things. I know he is a little broken. But he's my dad. He taught me how to climb a ladder. That's how I ended up on the roof in the first place that time I fell through the skylight. He showed me the way to get up high and see things from on top. He never said I couldn't do it. Because of him, I learned to see the most direct path and all the obstacles that stand between me and home.

What is my Why?

He's still my dad, and nothing anyone says or does can take that away. Not Bree and her meanness. Not my mom when she is sad and worried, and her anxiety fills me with dread, even I know she is just trying to take care of me. Not the rotten jerk who stole my laptop. Not Miss Pat and her twisty bruising fingers.

What is my Why?

When I have a bad day, forget important things and fail at important stuff, home is the only place I want to be. Because there's a plate of food in the fridge at midnight and, even though she pretends she doesn't, my mom watches me when I sneak outside onto the roof. Because even though my dad doesn't live with me anymore, he is still a part of the place that feels like home. The one that burned down. The tiny apartment. Even that room with only a mattress on the floor in the house he shares. Or the bed of the diesel truck with the bumper sticker that says, "My zombie ate your honor student."

Wherever he ends up, I want to know how to find him. I want him to know that I am okay and he should get better so we can be together again. I want him to know that *I am better.* Not perfect. Better.

I want him to meet my friends.

I know what to do. I didn't see it before, but now it's obvious. It was there all along. A running start for momentum, feet leave the ground, swing arms forward. This pushes me over the wall. Sitting position on the way down. My body feels heavy going down, but I'm prepared for the impact. I'm not headed for the ground. I'm aiming for the tree. When I hit the tree, my feet land on a branch and I stop myself by grabbing a branch above me. I sway a little then get my balance. It's still a long way down, but now I have a ladder. The tree is the way. I just had to clear some junk out of my head to see it.

From there it's an easy climb down to the lowest branch. I push off and land into a safety roll. Back up on my feet, no time to stop and congratulate myself. I've got a bus to catch. As I tear across the park at full speed, I know that I'm winning. I know that I will beat Freddy to my bus stop. I *know* it.

Freddy has already closed the bus door when I make it to 52nd Street and Maple Avenue. Lazy vault over the bench. Freddy sees me. He throws open the bus door.

"My word, I've never seen anything like that in all my life! Give this kid a hand, people!"

The entire bus cheers and claps for me. I grab my backpack from the seat.

Freddy says, "You have a great rest of your day, now, son."

I stop by the Hawaiian ice shop and get a rainbow ice. That's six flavors full of food coloring and high fructose corn syrup that my mom says I should not have. It's going to give me a headache, but I don't care. I know that I'm in trouble for leaving school. I know I should go home and call my mom and tell her I'm okay. I just want to enjoy my victory a little longer. The Hawaiian ice man recognizes me and gives me another coupon, for being a repeat customer.

It's square. I know exactly what to do with it.

When I make the call, Mom's voice answers, frantic.

"Jeremy? Are you okay? Dr. Nugent called and said you left school."

"Mom," I begin.

"Where are you?"

"Mom, listen."

"Tell me where you are, and I'll come get you."

"Mom. Stop. I'm fine. I'm home." It's quiet on the other end for a few seconds.

"Mom, I'm okay. I'm home. I'm sorry I scared you."

"I'll be there as soon as I can."

I shower, bandage my skinned palms and ice a bruised shin. I make a ham sandwich on gluten-free bread, thinking about what I am going to say.

She rushes in and drops her purse on the floor.

"What happened at school?" She asks, checking out the bruises.

Truth #1: There are no wrong answers. Just wrong questions.

"It's not what happened at school. It's what happened in my head."

"Jeremy," she begins. "We've talked about this and what goes on in your head. Sometimes things are harder for you than other kids."

Truth Number Two: Labels limit people.

From my pocket, I fish out the little paper crane I folded from the Hawaiian ice coupon and place it on the table.

"Did you know there is more than one way to fold one of

these?" Mom doesn't answer. She looks sad and worried. She drops her head and sighs.

"You don't have to stay there if you don't want to. We'll find another school. We'll figure this out, Jeremy. Just tell me what I can do to help you."

"Mom. No. That's not what I'm saying. Listen."

"Okay. I'm listening."

"There was this girl in Japan. She got radiation sickness from the Hiroshima bombing. She was going to die. She folded these cranes because there's a legend that if you fold one thousand paper cranes, your wish will come true. But she died before she got to one thousand. So, her friends finished for her. They made all the rest of the cranes."

Truth Number Three: Kindness Heals.

Mom says, "What are you trying to say, Jeremy?"

"Do you know what her wish was?"

She shakes her head and looks confused.

"Peace," I say.

"Jeremy," she starts. But I interrupt her.

"Mom. It was *peace*." I watch her face to see if she understands, but I can tell that she is still hung up on the wrong question.

"Mom, it's not the school that is wrong. It's not you, or my dad, or anything like that."

"Then what is it?"

"I need to do things my way. Without a label. Just being me."

"Okay," she says. "How can I help?"

"Encourage me. Like you always do."

CHAPTER 38

A TERRIBLE ACT OF WAR

Tully and Dr. Nugent sit across the table in the distraction-free conference room. Now I get why Trace calls the conference room the "chamber of horrors." It's where they take you when you first visit the school so they can observe your reaction. It's also where you go when your parents are summoned. Unlike the classrooms, it's bare and boring. Mom isn't here today. Tully talked to her on the phone about my running away from school. It's just me, Tully and Dr. Nugent. I ask for a piece of paper, and a pencil and Tully slides them over.

I draw a big circle that takes up almost the whole page. Then I start writing names inside.

Dad. Mom. Trace. Hazel. Jeremy the Younger. Freddy and Marie. Dr. Nugent. Tully. Mr. Turnbull. The entire Parkour class. I write them all in the circle. Everyone I can think of. Then I slide the paper to Tully.

Tully's face breaks into a big smile.

"Before you say anything, I have a plan. And I need your help." Tully and Dr. Nugent look at each other.

Dr. Nugent says, "Okay. We're listening."

Truth Number Four. Answers evolve.

Trace and Hazel are waiting for me.

"Are you okay?" Hazel asks excitedly. "Did you get in trouble?"

I look around the room until I spot Bree and Jeremy the Younger.

"Not exactly, but I think I have a way to fix Bree for good. Are you in?"

Trace practically does a front flip right there. Hazel's eyes get big.

"Oh yeah, we're in."

"There are two parts to this plan. The first part involves a lot of these," I hold up an origami crane in my fingers. "The second part," I pause and look around the room until I see Stanley.

"Hey, Stanley!" I call. He looks up from his book. "How many sticky notes do you think it takes to cover a locker door?"

"Thirty-two," Stanley says without hesitating.

"The second part will require at least thirty-two people willing to tell us their most awful secrets," I say.

"Not going to happen," Trace says.

Hazel looks doubtful. "What if we write them down with no names on them?"

"That might work," Trace agrees. "If we also bribe them with candy."

"Okay," I say. "We're going to need to be sneaky. But I have a secret weapon."

"What?" They both ask eagerly.

"Not what. Who."

A group of upper-level students is passing out stacks of paper to every table. Square sheets of paper, white on one side and colorful on the other. Origami paper. Dr. Nugent takes the stage and switches on the smart board. There's a folding diagram for an origami paper crane.

"Jeremy Johns, can you come up?" Dr. Nugent says.

I'm nervous. I don't like everyone looking at me. I don't like talking in front of people. But I get out of my seat and walk to the stage.

Dr. Nugent says into the microphone, "Jeremy is going to tell us the story of the peace crane and then you'll learn to fold your own. Our goal is to fold one thousand cranes, and Jeremy is going to tell you all about it."

My hands are shaking, and I feel like I could throw up, especially because Bree is seated right in front. I see Tully standing in the very back of the room. He has a big smile on his face. I focus on him until the rest of the room goes fuzzy.

"These are peace cranes," I say, my voice cracking. "And their story begins with a sick girl and a terrible act of war."

Dr. Nugent and Tully collect all the paper cranes. Stanley

estimates that out of the entire school of four hundred students, we collected seven hundred and fifty-two paper cranes.

"You are short two hundred and twenty-eight cranes," Stanley says.

"Close enough," I say.

Stanley disagrees. "I would like to be responsible for the remaining two hundred and twenty-eight."

I like Stanley. He is just so... Stanley. "That would be great." I hand him the remaining origami paper and off he goes.

Trace, Hazel, Ben, David, and Karmen huddle with me outside the MPR. Trace reaches around into his pack and pulls out Mr. Carpenter's bags of candy.

"You stole those?" Ben exclaims.

"He needs new ones anyway," Trace says.

"This has to happen fast before Bree gets suspicious, or Mr. C misses his candy," I say, handing out pads of sticky notes. "Get as many of these done as you can before lunch. Remember, no names, just secrets."

Nods all around. Hazel is so excited she jumps and squeals as we walk to first period.

It takes a lot of convincing to get kids to write down the one thing they won't even speak out loud. Most won't do it. We explain that it's to help someone, and the younger kids are cool with that, along with a fistful of jelly beans. But the kids in seventh grade and up, like us, are tougher. I finally tell them what it's all about. When I mention Bree, almost everyone takes a sticky note and a pen and writes.

We meet up at Dr. Nugent's office just before fourth period, holding bags stuffed with origami cranes and piles of sticky notes. Dr. Nugent hands me a little slip of paper.

"Peace be with you," she says.

It's Bree's locker combination.

CHAPTER 39

OPERATION PEACE CRANE

During Minecraft hour, Turnbull sends Bree out of the room to have her monthly check-in meeting with Tully and Dr. Nugent. When she is gone, Turnbull sends me a chat message.

Operation Peace Crane is a go.

That's our cue. Trace, Ben, David, and I slip out of the room, but not before Jeremy the Younger notices. He's already distressed that Bree left. He runs out into the hallway and slaps me on the arm.

"You're it," he says, angrily.

"I'm sorry, I can't play Jeremy Tag right now."

He slaps me again on the arm. Harder.

"You're it!"

"Dude," Trace says. "Let's just go."

But it's too late. Jeremy the Younger's face is full of hurt. Turnbull steps into the hall and calmly intercepts.

"Jeremy, I have something to show you, would you please come back in the room?"

"No! No! No!" He pushes Turnbull, even though he can't budge a much larger and heavier human, then throws himself against the wall. "No leaving me! No leaving!"

"Wow," I say. "Okay. Okay. Let's bring him with us."

"Are you crazy?" Trace says with astonishment.

"It might help him. I don't know. But this sure isn't helping him."

Turnbull looks troubled. "You sure?"

"Yeah. It's no fun to be left behind."

The three of us walk down the empty hall toward the lockers. Jeremy the Younger trails behind us, not talking and not smiling, but he also isn't hollering anymore. When we reach Bree's locker, I pull out the combination and open the lock. We dump as many of the cranes as we can fit inside, close the door and replace the lock. Jeremy the Younger watches us.

"That's Bree's," he says, over and over.

"It's okay," I assure him. "Here, take these and push them through the vents." He helps us push the remaining cranes into the vents on the locker until we've used them all up.

"Thanks to Stanley, we have at least one thousand," I tell Jeremy the Younger.

He smiles. "Bree gets her wish."

Trace and I look at each other.

"What's her wish?" I ask.

Jeremy the Younger replies, "Same as mine."

"We have to hurry," Trace urges. We hand Jeremy the Younger a stack of sticky notes.

"Put these on the locker door. Cover it all up, okay?" He nods and sticks. There are more notes than will fit on Bree's locker, so we stick them on the surrounding lockers. It's a big yellow sticky splatter of secrets.

When we are done, we step back and admire our work for a moment. Then I reach out and lightly tag Jeremy the Younger on the arm.

"You're it."

CHAPTER 40

FREAKS AND THEIR SECRETS

Trace, Jeremy, and I make it back to the Minecraft room just in time for the bell. Turnbull asks me how it went.

"The peace crane has flown," I say.

"Most excellent news," he responds with a wink.

The bell rings and doors fly open. Kids scatter loudly and crowd the hallway to get to their lockers.

My heart is racing, and I feel like I just made a terrible mistake. What if Bree doesn't get it? What if she reads everyone's secrets out loud and makes fun of them? It's possible she actually is a bully and will make things worse. And I'll be responsible. We gave everyone our word they would not be humiliated.

I shoot Trace a worried look, and he says, "Yeah. Me too."

Then I see Dr. Nugent at the end of the hallway. A hand claps my shoulder. It's Tully.

"Let's do this," he says. We walk together. Trace, Hazel, Ben, David, Karmen, and Jeremy the Younger catch up with us. I count them up. The most friends I've ever had at one time.

When we get to Bree's locker, students are milling around, curious. Some are reading the sticky notes. No one is laughing. In fact, it's surprisingly quiet. No one reads the secrets out loud or even touches the sticky notes like if they do the secrets will jump off the paper and take over their bodies.

No one wants these secrets. But everyone has one or more. All together we seem like a bunch of freaks, except when I look around, I don't see freaks. I see kids who are like me. Some have it even worse, and I never knew.

"I pull out my hair."

"I chew holes in my clothes."

"I can't tie my shoes."

"I steal things."

"I lie to everyone."

"I pick holes in my skin that bleed."

"I can't ride a bike."

"I'm afraid of stairs."

"I chew my fingernails. And toenails."

"I put my clothes on backward."

"I wear pull-ups at night."

"Sometimes I suck my thumb."

"I set fire to my house."

"My parents split because of me."

I put that one in about the fire. But that last one? That wasn't me.

No one laughs because everyone gets it. This isn't funny. I feel sick inside. I was wrong to do this. But Tully and Dr.

Nugent went along with it so it couldn't have been wrong, could it?

Bree approaches her locker. She hesitates as kids move out of the way. She looks around and sees her brother, who is between Tully and me. Then she sees her locker.

Slowly, she walks up to it. She picks a sticky note off and reads it silently. Then she puts it back. She takes another, reads it and puts it back. No one is moving or saying a word. Bree's head is down, and she stands very still for a moment. A long moment. The quiet hall is disturbing, and some kids shuffle around, uncomfortably. Tully takes a step forward and is about to say something when Bree turns to him quickly.

"No."

I think she's going to tear them all up. But she doesn't. She takes the notes one at a time and moves them from her locker onto the adjoining lockers. Then, her hands shaking, which I did not expect, she turns the lock combination and opens the door.

Jeremy the Younger can't stand anymore. He wails as the peace cranes tumble out of Bree's locker. She jumps back at first, startled. The cranes pool at her feet. So many cranes, crammed into every millimeter of locker space. She picks one up. She turns and looks at me. Then Bree does something no one thought she was capable of.

She starts to cry.

CHAPTER 41

EMPTY EYES

Hazel is the first one to run to Bree. Shocker, I know.

"It's okay," she says, throwing her arms around Bree. "It's okay. We just want to be friends."

At first, Bree stiffens and resists. Then she just gives up and hugs Hazel back. Trace elbows me.

"Women," he whispers with a smile.

Jeremy the Younger carefully approaches Bree, on his knees, picking up a handful of the cranes that are scattered all over the floor.

"Bree, your wish comes true now," he says excitedly.

Bree sniffles and sits back on her heels. She picks up a crane and studies it. Then she tips her hand and lets it fall to the floor.

"It's just paper," she says, sadly. "It doesn't change a thing, kid."

Jeremy the Younger looks crushed. Dr. Nugent steps in.

"Off to class now, everyone. Bree, let's go have a talk in my office. Everything is going to be okay."

Hazel, Trace, and I stay behind to sweep up all the cranes and take down the sticky notes. Jeremy the Younger stuffs his backpack with cranes before he leaves.

"Do you think she's right?" Hazel says. "Did we do all this for nothing? It doesn't change anything?"

Trace is scooping handfuls of cranes into a bag. "I'm not sure," he says.

I'm picking sticky notes off the lockers. This one interests me the most.

My parents split because of me.

It has a little person drawn on it with empty circles for eyes.

"Maybe," I say, "Maybe she wasn't talking about us at all. Maybe she was thinking about something else entirely." I show Trace and Hazel the note.

"I think this is her brother's," I say. Then I shove the note into my pocket. We finish cleaning up in silence and walk to class. I am still not sure if we just did a good thing or a terrible thing.

All day my stomach is knotted. I feel horrible. Worried. Trace and Hazel, too. We all shoot looks at each other that say, *I wish we hadn't done this.* But there is no undoing what's been done. I know that better than anyone.

When Bree doesn't show up for our last class of the day, I know for sure that there is something wrong and I need to fix it. I excuse myself to go the bathroom. I run to check the lockers. I go by Dr. Nugent's and Tully's offices to peek through the little windows. Empty. I check Room 3.14, the MPR, the chess board and the trampoline and the rock wall.

But I don't find Bree. Instead, she finds me.

CHAPTER 42

ALLIES

Bree grabs my arm and pulls me toward the front door of the school.

"Hurry!" she says urgently. "This way!" Then she takes off leaping down the front steps of the school.

"What's happening?"

"My brother!" She says frantically. "I'm such an idiot. I should have never told him."

I follow her running steps down the street toward the bus stop.

"He went this way. Why am I such a jerk?"

"Slow down, what happened?"

"You. It's your fault. You and your stupid cranes. He believed in it. And then I had to go and tell him the truth."

"What truth?"

Bree looks down the street. Then she points. "There. The bus. He asked me about the bus!" Bus Number Two is lumbering down the street about a block away. We both take off running. We're at the mercy of stoplights. The bus has a lead on us, and it just skims through a yellow light and halts at the bus shelter on the other side of the street. Traffic roars in front of us and I grab Bree's arm to stop her from running into the cars.

"Wait!" I yell. "What truth?"

"I told him that the divorce was temporary. That my parents would get back together," she says. "But it was all a lie. My dad bought a new house. We're going to live with him. This is all my fault."

Across the street, the bus pulls away after loading its passengers.

"Where is he going on the bus?"

"He's trying to go to our house. Our old house. Where we lived before the divorce. He wants to live there again."

"Where is it?"

"On the other side of the park. The light is changing!" We dash across the street, but the bus is already far ahead of us. I grab her arm.

"I know another way."

Bree is right on my heels as I run toward the Arizona Science Center. The center is packed this afternoon so we stay as high as we can, moving through the maze of people by running along the walls that snake through the complex. I can see the light rail station and the pedestrian bridge, the open-air market and just beyond that the parking garage. But we can't see Bus Number Two.

"We're losing it," she hollers as we land on the sidewalk between the science center and the light rail tracks, pausing to catch our breath.

"No, we're not." At the light rail station, people are queuing up to get on the approaching train. We go right behind them across the metal benches and dash across the track before the train pulls in.

At the pedestrian bridge, Bree takes the left side, and I take the right, and we bear-crawl up each side rail, rip across the bridge, and leap the downstairs, landing light on our feet. Bree's jump is better than mine. She beats me by a second or two and is already pointed toward the open-air market.

People are blurs as we thread our way through and up and over. It seems like they are standing still. I see the places I want to land and jump off again. Ahead, I can see the parking garage on the other side of the market. I holler to Bree, who sees it, too.

"On the other side! The bus will be there."

Cars are pulling in and out, driving up and down a ramp that winds through the center. I pause and look around me.

Bree sees it. "Come on!" she yells. She doesn't hesitate at all. She skims the roof of the cars to the center ramp, and we crawl up to the top level, where we are clear and open. On top of the garage, we scan for the bus. But it isn't there.

"No way, we couldn't have lost it already!" Bree says, hands on her hips and breathing heavy from the run. "This is three-stories high! I can't make that jump."

"Yes, you can," I tell her. "Watch me."

For the second time, I do the hardest thing I've ever done. Off the roof, land on the branch, swaying until I catch a branch to steady myself. Then down to the ground.

I hear the familiar squeal. We didn't lose the bus. We are ahead of it!

"Hurry!" I shout at Bree who is looking down at me.

"That was spectacular!" She hollers.

"Just jump!"

The branch creaks when she lands on it, and she loses her balance. Slipping off the branch, she grabs another. When she drops to the ground her legs are scratched and bleeding.

The bus pulls up. I wave at Freddy who looks startled. He hits the brakes and opens the door.

"Kid, you sure make my days interesting," he says. Then he gestures to the back of the bus. "I think someone could use a friend."

Bree doesn't bother with introductions. She jumps up the bus steps and runs down the aisle to her brother, who is sitting by himself in the very back, clutching his backpack. She approaches him like he's a terrified little animal that might take off running into the street. She doesn't say a word as she sits next to him. I take a seat on the other side. Jeremy the Younger leans into Bree and puts his head on her shoulder. A small sound escapes from her, and I realize she's trying not to cry. She doesn't want to make him any more upset than he already is.

When we get to my stop at 52nd Street, I get up to leave.

"My apartment is this way. We can call your mom," I say.

Bree stays seated. "Our old house is at the next stop," she says softly.

"You want to go there?"

She looks at her little brother's head on her shoulder.

"I don't think we have a choice."

I sit down and wave to Freddy, who nods and closes the bus door. We drive one more stop. It's an old neighborhood, full of tall trees and little brick houses with big windows and grassy front yards. Bree stands up.

"Jeremy, we need to go now." He doesn't look at either of us as he stands up and follows his sister up the aisle.

"You kids take care now," Freddy says. I offer him my hand.

"Thanks," I say. "You're a good friend."

He leans in and says, "As are you."

CHAPTER 43

FLYING

Jeremy the Younger scrunches his face up to the window glass in the front door of his empty house. Bree tries the door, but it is locked. Attached to the door handle is a black lock-box with a combination, so he begins to spin the numbers, attempting to break the code. There's a sign in the front yard that says "Sold."

Bree and I circle the house and try every door and window, but there is no way in. Jeremy the Younger is crouched on the front door mat when we return. He is unable to retrieve the key from the lock-box.

"Now what?" I whisper to Bree. She shakes her head. She kneels next to her brother.

"We need to call Dad." Her voice shakes. Her brother is locked up in every way imaginable. He cannot speak because there is an onslaught of words in his brain. He cannot hear because every tiny sound thrums in his ears. He cannot move because every limb wants to go in a different direction. He cannot see because every speck of light is an oncoming train. Jeremy the Younger is in a box of his own. I know exactly what that feels like. Sometimes, you can't get out of this box by yourself. Someone else must unlock it. Someone on the outside. They must be able to see that you are in there, but you can't talk to them right now. You need quiet time.

I'm searching my brain for an answer. I want to curl up in my own safe box, but I force myself to think. I think better when I'm moving so I pace up and down the front walk. Bree sits with her head in her hands next to Jeremy the Younger. I pace and pace and pace and then I see it unfold, one bit at a time, then all at once, it becomes map. A map into Jeremy the Younger's tangled brain.

I see a tree, with a branch like a wing, extended toward the roof of the house.

I see a house, made of red brick and pretty windows with a saddened roof covered with pine needles and dead leaves.

A roof pitched just right for observing the sky.

The sky, with stars and the weighted blanket of night beginning to fall.

I reach into my pocket and pull out a paper crane. I walk to Jeremy, crouch down, and hold out my hand, palm down, with the crane concealed in my fingers. I nudge his knee with my knuckles. He shakes his head at first. Then he peeks. His hand moves out from under his coat, toward my hand. When his fingers are under mine, I let the crane fall into his palm. He doesn't look at it. He just closes his fingers, pulls his arm back into his body and puts the crane in his pocket. Bree watches, her eyes full of tears. A small gasp of relief escapes her.

"Jeremy," I say in a calm voice. "Let's go on the roof and set it free."

Jeremy unfolds himself a limb at a time. We all move slowly. Up from the step. Slow walking because right now that is what Jeremy the Younger prefers. I lead them both to the tree.

"I've got this," Bree says. "I've done this a million times." Without another breath she runs at the tree like it is a wall, one foot landing on the trunk, her arms thrown forward to grab the limb and then she is up, crouched on the winged branch, extending her hand.

I help Jeremy unfold his arms and position his feet on the tree. I walk him through it slow-mo. When he has both feet on the trunk and both hands grasping a branch, I boost him while Bree pulls him. He lands on the branch, seat first. I see the first wrinkle of a smile on his face.

The branch is strong and holds us all. Bree is first to cross the five-foot gap between the tree branch and the roof. She takes two full strides and one long jump toward the roof, her arms thrown back then forward and up over her head, pulling her over the gap for a perfect landing. Jeremy the Younger whimpers and shakes his head.

"It's okay. We'll go like this," I move on all fours, like a crawling baby. He follows me until I stand on the branch, leaving just enough room to make a run at the gap.

"Can you jump?" I ask him.

He shakes his head no ferociously. "Not jump. Fly."

Bree calls to him, "Yes, fly! You can do it. Just like I did!"

Suddenly, Jeremy the Younger looks troubled again. "Backpack," he says. "I have more." It takes me a second to put it together. He has a backpack full of paper cranes.

"I'll get it." I swing down and run back to the front step for his pack.

When I come back to the tree, Bree is coaxing him into position. He stands up on the branch, his feet one in front of the other, while Bree counts to three.

Then he runs. Everything he has is running. Long leaps across the branch, just like he has done it a hundred times in his head. He pushes off the branch, and his arms go up, his feet come together, and he is in the air.

Jeremy the Younger is flying.

CHAPTER 44

RELEASE

Cushioned by the pine needles and leaves, we sit on the rooftop and count the stars as they come alive in the sky. For every newly appeared star, Jeremy the Younger releases one paper crane into the world. He holds a bird aloft in his hand against the backdrop of the sky, and we say goodbye to each one. Then we blow softly and watch it tumble, skittering across the roof, falling off the edge, or picked up in the breeze and transported somewhere else in the yard.

From my pocket, I pull out the one sticky note I took from Bree's locker. Jeremy the Younger leans over to look at it. He points to the figure with the empty eyes.

"Did you draw this?" I ask. He nods.

"That's Bree," he says.

"It's a good drawing. Should we fold this one too?"

"Please do," Bree answers. I hand it to Jeremy, and he begins to make a tiny paper crane out of the sticky note. He hands it to Bree. She holds it up in her hand and blows. The breeze catches it. In moments, it's gone.

When we see the lights of a police car approaching down the street, Bree reaches across her brother and grabs my hand. She gives it a squeeze and holds it tightly. My hand tingles in her warm fingers. Jeremy the Younger points to the police car as it slows and makes a few siren noises, then stops in front of the house. It's followed by three more cars.

"I'm suspended for a week," she says. "And disqualified from the summer camp contest."

"How did you do it? Get all that dirt on everyone?" Bree gives me a look like she ate a lemon.

"Oh, that. I get sent to Dr. Nugent's office frequently. And frequently she is pulled away to handle some other situation besides me."

"You hacked her computer?"

"What can I say? I have a gift. Plus, she once forgot to lock it when she was called away for five minutes. I can make magic happen in five minutes."

I take a deep breath and squeeze Bree's hand and then she lets go. Car doors fly open. A police officer talks into his radio while pointing to the roof. A man whom I don't know, my mom, Tully, and Dr. Nugent rush toward the house.

Mom loses it right away and starts crying. Dr. Nugent puts her arm around her. Tully waves and calls up.

"You kids okay?"

The officer looks for a ladder. Bree, the bravest of us, slides down to the edge of the roof and cat hangs down to the ground. Her dad hugs her and waves up to us. But Jeremy the Younger hides his head in his arms.

Tully walks around the yard, spots the tree, and gets himself right up on the roof with us. He sees paper cranes scattered on the roof and the yard. Then he sits down next to me, stretches out his legs and leans back on his elbows.

"Did you know there is a crane constellation?" Tully says. "It's named Grus. Latin for the crane. Cranes were sacred to Hermes. You know Hermes. Messenger of the Gods. Winged feet and all that. I like to think of Hermes as the original Parkour master."

Jeremy the Younger says, "Show me Grus."

"I wish I could, but it's only visible in the southern hemisphere."

We sit quietly together on the roof, watching the police officer and a neighbor carry a ladder across the yard and lean it up against the house. There is a flurry of voices down below, and I feel like I am just floating above them. I don't want to come down, and neither does Jeremy the Younger.

Bree is the first to climb up the ladder.

"Come on over here, Jer-Bear," she coaxes. "Dad says we can get pizza."

Jeremy the Younger first stuffs a handful of remaining cranes into his pocket, then slides on his seat down to the edge, where Bree helps him turn around and get his feet on the ladder. Their dad lifts him off before he gets to the ground and wraps him in a huge hug. He takes him to the car. Then he and Bree go to talk with the police officer.

It's just Tully and me now. My mom is calling my name. Asking me to please come down.

"Tully?" I say.

"Hmm?"

"There are so many reasons why."

He lets out a huge breath like he was holding it for two minutes.

"Gracious, yes."

"I can't choose only one why."

"No, you can't. I can't either."

"I think he needed to say goodbye. To his house. To things he loves," I say.

Tully looks up. "There are so many stars. So many things to love. They all can't stay. So, yes, sometimes we just have to say goodbye. But the reason you become who you are, that stays the same."

"Am I in trouble?"

"Heavens, no, Jeremy. Right now, you are in outer space."

That makes me laugh. "I guess I better go home."

We slide down to the roof edge and drop to the ground, Tully jumps down into a roll across the grass. I use a cat-hang. The neighbor who brought the ladder looks at us like we're crazy.

I wave to Bree and her brother as their dad drives them away. The backseat window goes down, and I see a small fist reach out and open. A handful of cranes flies out the window. Never to be seen again.

My mom hugs me like it is has been forever since I left, and I've changed so much she hardly recognizes me. I have so many things I want to tell her. Because I'm back from a journey. The journey to me. Like I've flown across the universe and back.

I guess, in a way, I have.

CHAPTER 45

FLIGHT OF THE CRANE

In the spring, we build a new course in Room 3.14. We call it The Zebra Challenge Course. Everyone contributes one obstacle from their own real-life experiences. Trace, Ben, David, and I prototype it in Minecraft. Bree and her brother help. It's our final exam.

Trace's part is the beginning: tilted quadrupedal steps. It's a set of square platforms turned at a 45-degree angle and staggered across the floor for the runner to crisscross. Trace calls it the Alligator Pond because, he says, every day for kids like us is like crossing a pond with only alligators to step on, trying to not be eaten alive.

Hazel adds a plank traverse that she names The Underbelly Exposure. One bar is high, and the other is low. Feet go on the low bar, hands on the high bar and you walk yourself across, your entire body slanted and facing the ground, or as Hazel explains it, exposing your most vulnerable self to the world below. It's a lot harder than it looks.

Karmen adds rings that she names the Circles of

Truth. These are suspended over a mat to swing from ring to ring, arm to arm, without falling into the Pit of Lies. It takes a lot of upper body strength.

Bree creates the Vault into the Unknown. It's a triangle foam vault, placed so that you cannot see what is on the other side. It's a trampoline, but you won't know that until you land on it. It's Bree's way of saying that we can trust her.

The next one is mine. It's The Burning House. From the platform starting point, you go down a fire pole. Then you go back up a cargo net. Then you come down a rope. Then you go up and over a wall. When you come down on the other side, you are right in the middle of the flames, represented by a staggered group of foam blocks placed far enough apart that each jump requires all your effort. If you fall into the fire, you start over at the fire pole.

Jeremy the Younger is invited to build an obstacle, as an honorary member of Room 3.14. He adds a set of swings. They are low to the floor, so you stand on them and step from one to the next while they are swinging. Like a flying trapeze, only a foot off the ground. He is very proud of it.

He calls it The Flight of the Crane.

CHAPTER 46

THE FIFTH TRUTH

It's Open House day. We can invite anyone, not just parents, so I invite Freddy and Marie. I ask my mom if we can invite my dad, but she doesn't answer.

Open House starts with a tour. We lead our guests to see each one of our classrooms and what we do inside. Mom loves the yoga balls in the math room. Marie wants to play with the tactiles in Mr. Turnbull's Distraction Station. Freddy's mouth drops open when we knock the "secret" code for the Minecraft room, and the door swings open to a darkened room with glowing screens, where a handful of kids are giving a demo of a Minecraft village.

Room 3.14 gets the most looks of awe. Trace, Bree and I give a demonstration of The Zebra Challenge course to a crowd who are seated in rows at the end of the gym. I'm worried about this part because people I don't know are going to be watching. Bree tells me her strategy for staying cool when there is an audience to witness your flub-ups.

"I pretend it's an angry mob chasing me," she says. "Then I'm all about being faster and stronger than they are. Plus, I give them all goofball names. Like booger face or stupid pie nose."

All three of us begin at a different part of the course when Tully gives us the cue, which is blowing into a kazoo. My first challenge is The Underbelly Exposure. This one requires a lot of core strength. These are the muscles that make or break a Parkour athlete. Great core conditioning means you are stronger all around, more precise and controlled and more flexible. All important things to have if you want to avoid injury and fall correctly.

I dive out of the Underbelly Exposure and pop up to The Circles of Truth. I'm facing the audience. I scan the faces. I check my gut. I'm not scared. I count the people who are here for me. Mom, Marie, Freddy.

But then I see a face that wasn't there earlier.

It's my dad. He is sitting next to my mom. My heart is pounding now because surprises always throw me off. I move on to The Circles of Truth. These are tricky because they move around, like everything that is true, they can be approached more than one way. When I finish the course with The Alligator Pond, my dad is still there. When we all line up and bow like Olympians to a cheering crowd, my mind races the course, again and again, revisiting that moment I saw my dad's face in the audience. Hoping he will still be there.

After we finish the demo and our tour, I walk back to the MPR with my mom and dad, one on each side of me, and

Freddy and Marie behind us, chatting with each other. Dad and I talk like he never left. He tells me about his new job as an air conditioning repairman. He has his own apartment. Tully is on the stage ready to give one of his exuberant talks. Hazel is at the door handing out fidgets and calmers to anyone who wants one.

"Pipe cleaner? Stress ball? Chewing gum?" She has a basket full of items that are chewable, squishy or maneuverable. She holds out her hand to me.

"Here, I saved this for you." It's a bottle cap. I slip it into my pocket.

"Thanks, Hazel."

We all sit in the front, down a few seats from Trace and Hazel and their parents. When Tully takes the stage, the lights go off, and he launches into his *Don't just be the zebra, be the stripes* presentation. He explains the five truths and how we embark on a quest to live each one.

When the lights come on, Dr. Nugent and all the teachers join him on the stage.

"Now is the time that we recognize a student who had fully embraced the methodology of Equator School."

He explains that it is a very hard task to choose just one, how everyone has made astonishing progress, grades and scores are higher than ever, and every single student at Equator is a point of pride for Tully and his team.

"But there is one student that we would like to recognize. This person made decisions and took steps that not only changed his outcome but the outcomes of others," Tully says. "We are all better educators and better zebras than we were when Jeremy Johns came to Equator this year. Jeremy, please come up."

I have forgotten about the contest. Like so many things that were always unattainable—invitations to parties, best friends, good grades—I pushed it out of my thoughts. Tully coaxes me, and my dad gives me a little nudge. For him, I stand up and go to the stage.

"Congratulations, Jeremy. You not only earned your own stripes, but you also helped others find theirs. In the spirit of the award, we added a twist. Jeremy not only receives an all-expenses-paid Parkour summer camp, but he also gets to choose another student to bring along."

I'm nervous. I scan the faces of my friends who are all sitting up front. Trace, Hazel, Stanley, Gemma, Karmen, Ben, and David. I want to take all of them with me. Trace became my friend on the first day of school, even before I knew what a real friend is. Hazel helped me find my voice when I was afraid to use it. Stanley showed me how to look at things differently— way differently. Gemma and Karmen made me feel like a big brother. Important and needed. Then I look at Bree and her brother sitting next to their dad. Bree isn't looking at me. She is staring out the window. I wonder, and I'm sure she wonders, where is her mom right now? And the even bigger question: Why isn't she here?

I see my dad in the audience and think that the answer is there, somewhere, in the fact that my dad is sitting next to my mom, and even though I don't know what that means, whatever comes next, it's going to be okay.

Then it happens. The answer just comes to me, like landing a perfect precision jump.

I whisper to Tully, "I have a question," and he leans in and listens.

"Please, I think it's the right thing to do."

"Well, holy smokes, I—okay. This is a first for me, but I've learned that the unexpected is the norm with these incredible kids. Bree and Jeremy Callaway, would you please come up?"

From the back of the room, Bree looks startled. She stands up slowly and whispers to her brother, and they walk to the stage together.

Bree says under her breath as she stands next to me, "What are you doing?"

"Wrong question," I whisper back. "Not what. Why."

Tully pauses and looks at me. "Now, you're sure this is what you want to do?"

"I'm sure."

Tully turns to Bree and Jeremy the Younger.

"Jeremy has asked to forfeit his prize and send the two of you to Parkour camp," Tully says.

The audience is silent for a second then claps and hollers so loud that Jeremy the Younger buries his face against Bree and covers his ears. Tully motions to the quiet the room.

Bree wraps her arm around her brother. Her brother wraps his arms around her. Then Bree turns and hugs me. And it isn't weird.

CHAPTER 47

PEACE

I walk to the parking lot with my dad, and we sit in the cab of his truck while Mom is talking to Bree's dad. My dad says has something to give me. I have things I want to tell him. I have questions that I can't forget, even though I've tried. Like why did he go away the night of the fire? Why did he disappear and reappear and then disappear again? And the big question: Is he coming home? But I don't ask or tell anything. Because he pulls out a box from under the seat and hands it to me. It's a new laptop.

"I know this doesn't make up for everything that's happened, but I hope it helps. At least we can hang out again, you think?"

I am quiet for a long time. So many things are buzzing in my head and want to come out of my mouth. I can think of only one way to quiet the noise. I can think of only one way to make him understand how I feel.

I open the truck door and say, "I want you to see something." We both climb out of the truck and stand in the parking lot. He looks uncomfortable.

"Dad, listen, you have to commit. Even though it's scary. And there are a lot of steps," I tell him. "If something goes wrong, you abort into a break fall. It might knock the wind out of you, but you'll recover."

Then I show him what I've learned. I punch into my jump from the ground, eyes to the sky for the most height, tuck forward with my shoulders while thrusting up my knees, then tip my head forward.

Jump. I wish for friends.

Tuck. I wish I was smart.

Rotate. I wish I was normal.

Land. I wish my dad was here.

When I hit the ground on my feet, Dad is there, smiling, an arm's length away.

The world is still and quiet for a perfect moment. I stay in it as long as I can. It's warm like a heavy blanket. It's the stars viewed from the rooftop. It's the shivering leaves telling me a storm is coming. A drop of water on my head that inspires an answer. A sheet of crisply folded paper with movable wings. It's all that remains when the noise drops away.

It's *peace*.

And love made it happen.

A NOTE FROM THE AUTHOR

This story belongs to my son, Alexander, who was diagnosed with ADHD Inattentive Type, Obsessive Compulsive Disorder, and anxiety at the age of 13. He was also found to be gifted non-verbally. This is a condition known as twice-exceptional: the diagnoses of one or more learning disorders along with giftedness. Co-morbid conditions such as OCD, dyslexia, anxiety and autism spectrum disorders often accompany ADHD. On its own, ADHD presents a largely misunderstood struggle and a lifelong challenge. For gifted kids, it's an additional cruel reality.

This book is an experiment intended to occupy a safe space in children's literature for twice-exceptional learners to read about characters who share their unique struggles. It is also intended to give kids and parents hope that these kids can create their own successes, build strong relationships, form alliances and advocate for their needs. It is for gifted children who read far above their grade level but are too young or too sensitive to enjoy literature written for the young adult audience.

I welcome and encourage all feedback from readers and their parents so that I can improve my writing for this audience and help other writers do the same. I believe that we need to make a space in the canon of literature for kids who need main characters with whom they can connect intellectually and emotionally; characters who find a way to turn the curse of twice-exceptionality into positive outcomes. Feedback from children and those who care for them will help other writers who share this goal to improve and create even more stories for them to enjoy.

I hope you will join this endeavor. I understand this is a big ask, on top of all the many ways you support your twice-exceptional learners. I know you feel exhausted, discouraged and isolated. I know you feel hopeless when the world doesn't understand our kids and the odds are stacked against them. Change *is happening* in new schools created specifically for the twice-exceptional and teachers are beginning to learn how to teach them. We have a long way to go but *the world needs our kids*. The world needs their brilliance, their kindness, their unique way of solving problems and so many more traits that make them truly, and wonderfully, exceptional.

I want to leave you with one thought that I have carried with me every day of my life as an advocate for the rights of the disenfranchised. Let's mobilize and work together.

"Never doubt that a small group of thoughtful, committed citizens can change the world; indeed, it's the only thing that ever has." — Margaret Mead

ACKNOWLEDGMENTS

This book became a reality because of the unwavering support of my three twice-exceptional children, Alex, Isabel, and David. Despite many setbacks, disappointments and obstacles at every turn, your love, encouragement, and strength saved me from losing hope.

Alexander gave me permission to share his story. While much of it is fictionalized, the core story reflects his struggles, his triumphs and his remarkable ability to independently create positive outcomes for himself, from winning a scholarship to a Parkour camp to landing his first job at a Boy Scouts summer camp.

Thank you to Tempest Freerunning Academy in Los Angeles, who gave Alexander a summer he will never forget. As you have done for countless others, you gave him an experience that truly put him on a better path for his future.

Thank you to my lifelong friends, Jocy Schultz, Adam Beechen and Elissa Gillespie. You gave me someone to talk to when I needed it most and never let me forget what matters most.

Thanks to my writing companion and treasured friend, Mary DeRosa Hughes, after countless meet-ups at the bar counter of Changing Hands Bookstore, you helped me overcome my greatest fears and doubts that come with being a writer.

To the members of the Facebook groups and your children who first inspired me to even think about writing this book, then provided invaluable feedback as I progressed: you are all heroes. This would not have been possible without each one of you.

A special shout out to Harrison Becker, a twice-exceptional youth who became my first official reader. I'm deeply appreciative for your help and encouragement.

Finally, thank you to Kurt Krause, my hero and husband, for keeping me focused and grounded. You gave my children and me a life and home we would have never had without you. My deepest love always.

About the Author and Resources

Susan Krause is a marketing professional and writer raising three twice-exceptional children. She is an Arizona native and an advocate for the needs of gifted and 2E children. *Background Noise* is her first novel.

Contact her at susan@backgroundnoisebooks.com and follow her blog at backgroundnoisebooks.com

How to Get Involved:

Participate in discussions about literature and writing for gifted and 2E children, by joining the Facebook discussion group **Background Noise: Books for Gifted & Twice-Exceptional Youth.**

fb.com/groups/backgroundnoisebooks

Follow the Facebook page @Backgroundnoisenovel

Follow on Twitter: @2Ebooks

Join Facebook groups about giftedness and twice-exceptionality. Here are just a few:

- Raising Poppies
- Twice-Exceptional Children 2E
- Twice-Exceptional Kids Group

64514342R00155

Made in the USA
San Bernardino, CA
22 December 2017